A whale

for Libby

enjoy :)

Rachael Lindsay

2014

A note from the author

When I was a very little girl, I made an earwig farm with my best friend.
I thought I knew which were lady earwigs and which were the gentlemen. We used twigs and leaves to make them happy and we were so very gentle with them all.
I wanted them to have baby earwigs and so we sat down to wait…

And wait…

And then we gave up and had an ice cream.
I'm not sure if I washed my hands first…

I decided then that this baby thing takes time.

That's what makes all babies so special.

As every mother knows.

OF PIPES AND POTIONS

RACHAEL LINDSAY

OF PIPES AND POTIONS

Nightingale Books

NIGHTINGALE PAPERBACK

© Copyright 2010
Rachael Lindsay

A CIP catalogue record for this title is
available from the British Library

The troll-figurine on the cover page is an original Ny Form troll.
You will find all the Ny Form trolls at www.trollsofnorway.com

ISBN: 978 1 903491 93 5

Nightingale Books is an imprint of
Pegasus Elliot MacKenzie Publishers Ltd.
www.pegasuspublishers.com

First Published in 2010

Nightingale Books
Sheraton House Castle Park
Cambridge England
Printed & Bound in Great Britain

Dedication

Foor mi lovelor Mummy, Dorothy ~
Oor speshy, strongish dearig.
U shtay in oor hartlis.

Thanken, thanken foor everythingor.
Kissig, kissig.

Glossary

A

animor/es – animal/s

B

backen – back

backen-scratchli – back-scratcher

(screw-driver)

badli – bad

baskettli(s) – basket(s)

bi – by

biggy – big

boot – boat

C

catchen – catch/to catch

choppen – (to) chop

comli – come/to come

D

dearig(s) – dear/dear one(s)

dee – the

dedden – deadly/dangerous

doggor – dog

dreamoori – dreamer/dream/dreaming

drinkoosh – drink/to drink

dursty – thirsty

E

eatig – eat/eating/to eat

en – and

es – it's/is

everythingor – everything

F

fastli – quick/ly

fior – fire

findor – find

flaggermuss(es) – bat(s)

foor – for

foresh – forest

freezorig – freezing

G

goingor – going/to go

gooshty – good

gunnig – gun

H

hab – have

halloo – hello

happenig – happening

hartlis – hearts

helpen – help

Herbie Poshtig – collecting pouch

(usually for herbs)

homerig – home

hor – how

hungeror – hungry/hunger

hurtig – hurt

I

Im – I'm

J

K

kissig – kiss

L

leggor(s) – leg(s)

littelor – little

looki – look

lovelor – lovely

luckor – luck/lucky

M

marvellurg – marvellous

mattoori – (the) matter

meer – me

mekken – making/to make

menor – men/people

mi – my

missig – missing

Mistig Vorter – Misty Water (Thom's boat)

mooch – much

morgy – morning

morsi/es – mouse/mice

N

nay – no

nics – not

O

oop – up

oor – our

oos – us

outen – outside

P

peepor(s) – pipe(s)

pleasor – please

pleasorig – pleased

poshtig – bag/pocket

Q

R

reddig – ready

restig – rest/sleep

S

sadli – sad

scratchli – scratch/to scratch

secresht – secret

Shloopish – sleeping potion

shtay – stay

shtuk – stuck

sistoori – sister

sitli – sit/to sit

speshy – special

starterig – start

stoofid – stupid

strongish – strong

T

tay – tea

thanken – thank you

todagen – today

trickoori – tricky/difficult

troddler(s) – young troll(s)

tvo – two

U

u – you

ub – but

ur – your

V

varken – wake

ve – we

ver – where

verisht – very

vorter – water

W

walloo(s) – whale(s)

warmoosh – warm

wass – what's/what

willen – will

wit – with

wooden – wood

worrish/t – worries/d

X

Y

yo – yes

Z

So let's begin ~

All mothers know when the time is right.

From the mountain goat feeding on alpine grasses and flowers, to the scarlet macaw nesting in emerald tree tops of the rain forest.

From the polar bear curled in her sheltered snow-den, to the fleet-footed gazelle on the African savanna.

From the three-spined stickleback ready to lay eggs on the river bed, with her red-bellied mate zig-zagging over them, to *this* mother…

…who knew the time was right.

Ten long months before, she had begun to grow the new life which she now had to share with the world. The depths of the ocean had been icy-cold in the early spring, but the thought of her baby glowed within her and she swam with a serene beauty, instinctively seeking warmer waters.

How long she had waited!

Nearly time now.

She had delighted in every twitch, then every wriggle and then every turn of her young calf, as she embraced the wonder of it all.

Nearly time now.

How he had grown inside her, this little finner, nudging at her belly, keen to swim alongside her.

Nearly time now.

For weeks, she had driven her tail flukes up and down through fathoms, supporting him and propelling them towards this birthing water.

And now the time was right.

With a sudden rush and a swirling of the sea, with a push of her form and a twist of his –

with one final **thrust** and a *flurry* of confusion –

the young minke whale was flippered up, up, to the surface for his first breath of salty air.

Chapter One

*O*ne final ***thwack!***

One last log was chopped and tossed onto the pile with the others. The old she-troll dropped her ancient axe and slowly straightened her bent shoulders. Her panting breath made foggy clouds in the icy air and her cheeks were ruddy with exertion. She looked over to the shabby, wooden shack that was home and called to her sister.

"Halloo, Dotta! Looki – animores' wooden!"

When there was no reply, she wiped her strong hands on her red apron and strode to the doorstep.

"Halloo!" she called once more and shoved one hairy troll foot against the door to open it. There was a shudder and a weary creak of aged pine as the troll peered inside.

A smell of wood smoke and melted cheese wafted towards her. Two rocking chairs were facing the glowing fire and a steaming pot was dangling above it. Whilst the simple wooden bunk beds were blanketed with rough goat-hair covers, the feather pillows were plumped up softly and looked snug. The floor was swept and everything was in order.

And there was Dotta, of course, sitting at the table. She was so absorbed in what she was doing that she had neither heard her sister's call nor noticed the opening of the door, despite the rush of winter air that accompanied it. The abandoned baby wolverine in her arms guzzled noisily at the bottle of goat's milk, sucking more than he could swallow so it dribbled down his fluffy chin and dripped onto Dotta's lap. The gentle troll's face gazed adoringly at the cub, lost in thought. The other animals were settled and either snoozing or grooming, or playing tip-tap with each other. The weak ones were still resting in their wooden boxes filled with straw.

Grimhildr and Dotta had lived like this for so many years, they had lost count. The two had set up home together when the third sister, Hildi, had troll-married and decided to live with Thom in another part of the forest. As young trolls the three had been inseparable, growing up and learning essential skills from their elders. They knew the paths through the forest, the moods of the water down in the fjord and how to read the weather from nature's signs. They had learned to avoid the Big People, apart from essential trading with the few whom they could trust. They understood plants, animals and troll ways of life. They were loyal and loving.

Dotta had never met a strong troll-man, like Hildi had. She had long since given up hoping she might be married, but still yearned for troddlers. She had a natural affinity for every young animal she came across in the forest. They trusted her implicitly, no matter how wild they were, so that whenever they were in need, Dotta was the one they sought. She cared for the wounded and sick, the lonely and unloved, large and small. Her compassion knew no bounds.

Grimhildr shook her head and smiled at the sight of her sister-troll with the wolverine. There she had been, thwacking and chopping and sawing in the raw cold, whilst Dotta had been rocking and humming in the warmth!

"Dotta – gooshty wooden foor animores," Grimhildr called from the doorstep. "Looki!"

Dotta blinked suddenly, her day-dreaming disturbed, and turned her head. Her sister indicated the stack of wood piled up outside and mopped her brow.

"Oh! Verisht gooshty, Grimhildr! Thanken, thanken!" she exclaimed and, scooping up the bundle of grey fluff, got to her feet. Her rough shift was covered in animal hairs and dribbles of goat milk, but her dimples smiled and her eyes shone, making her old troll face quite lovely. She knew that Grimhildr had been working hard. Grimhildr always did.

…her dimples smiled and her eyes shone,
making her old troll face quite lovely…

The wood was essential to make boxes and beds for her animals. Other smaller pieces were valuable kindling for the fire which Dotta tended, keeping the tumble-down shack warm, day and night. Supple twigs and sticks were fashioned into woven baskets to carry the sick or wounded forest animals, or to trade with the Big People. Dotta even played dreamy, lilting tunes on tiny, carved wooden pipes.

Like all trolls, Dotta and Grimhildr were self-sufficient, living a simple life amongst the other forest dwellers. They hid away from the people of the town, knowing that they were often cruel and would take delight in destroying all they held dear. The mountain goats which had joined them, having left their cold craggy ledges in search of gentle care, provided endless supplies of milk. This was used to nourish the fostered animals until they were strong enough to return to their forest or rocky homes, and resume their life in the wild. It was also made into cheese and yogurt; the cheese often smoked or with added herbs, the yogurt flavoured with Hildi's honey or wild blueberries when in season. Dotta was proud of her dairy skills. She stacked her cheeses in a special cold shelter made by Grimhildr, where they kept fresh. Often she would give away tasty treats to other trolls and, in return, would receive smoked fish, baked bread or gathered mushrooms. The trolls did not have money. They did not need it. They cared for each other and lived the ancient life of their forefathers and mothers.

This winter, it was more important than ever that they should look after each other. The swan-silver snow had started earlier than usual, dusting the trees of the forest and settling in marble sheets on the mountain sides. The fjord water was dark and still, under a leaden sky. Icicles hung from the cold cheese shelter and the ground was frozen hard. The trolls had grown their winter fur down their backs, on troll tails and feet; essential protection from the elements. They all knew this winter was going to be tough.

~~~

A Big Man looked out of the window of his house and thought he might just have enough time to go out before the next snowfall. He had spent a considerable length of time shovelling the drifts from his path this morning so that his door could be kept clear, and he had an ache from hunger which would be ignored no longer. He returned to the fire he had lit earlier and reached down for his great boots, now dry once more and warmed. After pulling them on over his thick socks, laces yanked tightly, he picked up the half-cocked gun which rested against a cupboard. As he did so, his faithful dog pricked up her ears and began to thump her tail on the worn hearth rug. She saw all the signs of a hunting trip. They both knew that there was no fresh meat to be found in the town, and fish was in short supply. The bad weather had prevented normal trading and transport; the sea had been too rough for the boats to venture out. Dry biscuits, stale bread and mouldy cheese were all that remained in the food cupboards. Man and dog needed a meal, preferably a warm one, preferably with meat. Preferably before nightfall.

...his faithful dog pricked up her ears and began to thump her tail...

A thick, padded jacket hung on the hook by the door. A fur-lined hat and an enormous pair of gloves were stuffed into the pockets. They were stiff, cold and damp from this morning's work, but Halvor had no choice but to wear them again. He slapped his thigh in encouragement to the dog and his faithful friend left the warmth of the fire to stand at his side. With a scruffle of the dog's soft fur and a bone-chilling opening of the door, both were ready for the forest.

The biting wind caught their breath as they looked down the path, and then the road, and then the winding way through the trees. With a bit of luck, they would make it there and back within two hours and they would have at least a hare for the pot. With a lot of luck, maybe a deer to keep them going over the next few weeks. With no luck, perhaps only a squirrel or… nothing at all.

~~~

After a tasty meal of melted goats' cheese, Grimhildr and Dotta smiled happily. Unlike the Big People, they were warm and full.

"Im goingor mekken baskettlis foor animores, Dotta," Grimhildr announced. The animals' baskets and boxes needed replacing frequently to ensure they were in good order for any new patients. They were made in all sorts of shapes and sizes, for all sorts of shapes and sizes of animals, and each took a few hours to complete. It suited Grimhildr to have this sort of work. She enjoyed the outdoor life and needed to be bashing and building, working her strong, stocky body in the fresh air.

Dotta was pleased to think she would have the workroom inside to herself. She had seen to the immediate needs of the animals and wanted to try to make her special sleeping potion. Sometimes, the two trolls had to help an animal who was in pain and could not stay still. This would be a lot easier if the animal had a short sleep, so splinting and bandaging could be done more easily.

However, there was a problem with this.

A big problem.

Dotta was a bit dotty and wasn't too sure how to do it.

She had tried a few times now, with varying degrees of success. She had collected herbs in her Herbie Poshtig and dried them, chopped them, mixed them and changed the recipes. Like a true scientist, she needed to test her results – but didn't want to experiment on the animals – so she tested them on herself. Frequently.

Which probably explained quite a lot.

Dotta was a bit of a dreamer.

It was a good job that Grimhildr was there to keep an eye on her at times.

~~~

The piercing wind bit at their noses and stung their eyes. Halvor and his gundog pressed on into the forest, alert for any sign of movement amongst the shivering trees.

"Won't be long, Kishi," the man muttered in reassuring tones. Neither of them wanted to be out longer than necessary today. Although there were still a few hours of daylight left, the sky was becoming darker with the threat of more snow. Kishi padded closely alongside her master, chocolate-brown eyes searching for a flash of dinner. She slowed her pace to match his as the forest thickened and became more silent. The snow was thin on the ground just here, as most of it was caught up in the conifer branches, lacing them together in frosted icing. No animals were to be seen in this still world. Their underground burrows were snug hideaway places. The hares had wrapped their long ears around their long feet; the squirrels had curled up tight into their tails of fluff.

Halvor chose a change of direction.

A veering off the well-worn path through a lesser known part of the forest.

Here, the wild animals would not expect to see a man with his dog. Here, they would be free to roam without as much care for their safety. Here, lay the smaller paths of the trolls. And the tiny shimmer-trails of the fae creatures.

The hunters made no sound. Stealthily, they progressed further and further, Kishi's heart beginning to pound in expectation. The only sign of their presence was misty breath in the chilly air.

Suddenly, the Big Man stopped in his great-booted tracks. He strained to look through the shadows of the trees.

Had that been a flash of white, or was it just snowfall?

Was it the tail of a deer slipping silently from view?

One... more... step. A turn of the head. To listen.

The gun was cocked. Click.

~~~

Dotta inhaled deeply as she stirred the bubbling brew. She closed her eyes to appreciate fully the heady scent and began to sway slightly on her hairy feet. Her apron ties floated backwards and forwards, dangling perilously close to the flames of the kitchen fire as she hummed her favourite troll tune. In this particular mix she had put the usual honey and liquorice root-base, but had added some sweet, hay-scented chamomile and a little dried dandelion, plucked during the previous cool summer on the slopes to the fjord.

She would bubble and cool it, then try it this evening.

Hmm, hmm.

Bubble and cool.

Hmm, hmm.

Bubble and cool.

Hmm, hmm.

The dreamy fragrance suddenly changed. Dotta stopped her humming and slowed her swaying. Something was not quite right. She sniffed cautiously, eyes still closed.

No, not right at all.

In fact, very *wrong*.

Dotta sniff-sniffed again. And stopped her swaying altogether.

Now what was that familiar smell?

It reminded her of… reminded her of… what was it?

Smoky bonfires! That was it!

But that was so wrong!

With a sudden jerk, Dotta came to her senses and pinged open her eyes.

Smoke meant fire!

Sure enough, her apron ties had caught in the flames and an orange snake was creeping upwards, flickering its fiery tongue.

"Nay! Nay!" Dotta shouted out in fright, wafting her hands about, smacking at her little hairy legs. "Grimhildr! Fior! Fior! Grimhildr, helpen meer!"

With a *bang!* the door was flung open and her sister came to the rescue. Again.

~~~

At that very same moment, with a very different *bang!* the Big Man fired his gun blindly into the forest darkness, hoping that with luck, it would reach a target. Any target would do: rabbit, hare, fox, red squirrel. Anything he could possibly eat that night. He hoped, above all, that he *had* seen the tail of a deer flash, but he really couldn't be certain. And now that the gun had fired, any animal in the area would have fled, so this had been his one chance to kill for the pot.

"Go, Kishi! Go!" he urged and sent his excited dog in the direction of his shot. "Go fetch, girl!"

Kishi needed no further encouragement. With a joyful bark, she sped off and vanished into the trees, hoping to pick up the scent of blood. Halvor stood waiting for her return. He listened carefully to the sounds of the forest, knowing that as soon as Kishi had success, she would let him know.

So he waited.

And he waited.

He shuffled from one numbing foot to the other and strained to listen in the gathering gloom of dusk.

And he waited.

"Kishi?" he called in a low voice. "Kishi, girl?"

Nothing.

"Here, girl!" He called more loudly. "Come back, Kishi!"

Not a sound.

The Big Man took a step forward and this time he shouted, hands cupped around his bearded mouth.

"KISHI! HERE, KISHI!"

Then he heard, from a long way off, a howl.

A pained, mournful howl.

It made his blood run cold.

Then silence.

Galvanised into action, he lumbered through the undergrowth, searching desperately through gorse and bracken, yelling until he was hoarse. He crashed through the icy trees and frozen scrub, until night closed in.

"KISHI! WHERE ARE YOU?"

No answer.

No loyal Kishi.

Nothing to be seen or heard.

Exhausted and despondent, Halvor finally gave up and sorrowfully, with shoulders slumped and gun trailing, made his way home.

Two bats, with high pitched squeaks, flitted overhead.

~~~

And so it was ~

The minke whale calf was born into shallow waters but deep into his mother's fervent love. From his very first breath, he knew tenderness, safety and protection, and the glorious freedom of the open sea. Within half an hour of his birth, he could swim, learning to dip and dive and blow and breathe at his mother's side. Nutured with rich milk, the minke began to grow, bluish-grey in the sapphire depths. He was a miniature version of his mother in every way, just one third her size, except that his white flipper patch was a clear diamond, identical to his father's.

His mother adored him.

She knew she had one year to teach him about life in the ocean, before he would want to leave her and find his own way in the world. He must learn to be strong and independent. Just like every mother's child.

Chapter Two

*S*critch-scratch! Scritch-scratch!

The scritter-scratter at the cracked window of the little shack made Grimhildr and Dotta look up. The night was inky; the forest was dark and silent.

"Mi dearig flaggermusses!" Dotta cried with pleasure and went to let the bats in. "Halloo, Pipi en Fug! Comli in homerig en sitli bi fior. Es freezorig in foresh."

The bats hesitated for a moment, sniffing the air with their twitchy snouts, and then, deciding all was in order, they clambered over the sill, gripping with their small, clawed thumbs. With one quick swoop, each was in the cosy room ready for their evening with the trolls.

Pipi was a tiny pipistrelle with a plain nose and mousey eyes. She was covered in fine brownish-red fur on her back. Her underside was cream, and soft as velvet to the touch of Dotta's gentle finger. She, like her matey Fug, should have been in hibernation just now, but they were two very confused little rescue bats. Having been cared for when injured years ago, they were both reluctant to give up the warmth and love of the trolls' home.

Fug had been the first of the two patients. He was a common little brown bat, a little bigger than Pipi, with dark, glossy fur on his back. He had misjudged a swoop when flying over the cold water of the fjord, on a night rampage for insects, and had been doused. Thom had found him, coughing and spluttering, when he was finishing some repairs to his boat, Mistig Vorter. He had scooped up the bedraggled, skinny little bat and brought him tenderly to Dotta. She had cared for him, lovingly feeding him with moths and beetles, and he had bedded down amongst baby squirrels fallen from their tree. When he was ready to return to his roost, he took some persuading and now was a regular night-time visitor, even when other bats were hibernating in the cold winter months.

Pipi had been found by Grimhildr one day on the forest floor. She was only a few days old and had obviously lost grip of her mother during an early evening flutter. She was weak and needed round-the-clock tending to grow to her tiny adult weight. She had bonded well with Fug because, although shorter and lighter, she had larger ears and was much better at catching sounds when flying at night. This meant that together, they looked after each other and had left their colonies in favour of living with the trolls most of the time.

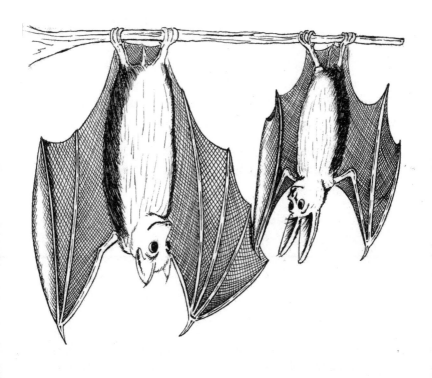

Fug   *Pipi*

Dotta, with her troll intuition, had learnt to understand their high-pitched squeaks. She could even call them with a shrill peep of her pipes, and was often the first to know what was happening in the forest and mountain caves simply by tuning in to their bat-speak. Tonight was no different.

"Doggor in foresh?" she questioned, looking across to Grimhildr with some concern. The bats climbed up the side of her chair, Dotta carefully not rocking to allow them steady grip.

"Gunnig doggor?" she asked. A gundog in the forest could only mean one thing; a hunter had been on the prowl!

The bats settled themselves, hanging upside-down on either side of Dotta's rocker, and continued their squeakings. With growing concern, the trolls heard about the shot fired, the Big Man crashing through the undergrowth, and how he had called and called for his hound.

"Missig doggor, nics gooshty," muttered Grimhildr. She knew how loyal gundogs were and that they would never go missing without good reason. The bats didn't seem to know any more. They seemed to be more concerned with practising their swinging and nibbling knobbly bits in their fur. This was the trouble with bats. No matter how much Dotta questioned them, they had no more to say. She fed them some gnats she kept in a jar and gave up. They would have to see what happened tomorrow.

As the fire began to die down to glowing red embers, one-by-one, all in the trolls' home began to sleep. The cobweb wolverine, full of warm goat's milk, dozed. The partridge tucked her head under her good wing, keeping her splinted wing straight. The two old badgers snuffled together, licking each other's healing wounds. All were peaceful – except for Pipi and Fug who left their perches to flit between the rafters catching the gnats that had got away.

~~~

Halvor sucked the end of his pen. Before him, on the table was a large, tatty sheet of paper. Writing was tricky but he was determined to do his best.

> Hav yu seen mi dog?
>
> She iz losst in the forez.
>
> She iz mi frend and I miz her.
>
> Corl Halvor if yu no enyfing.

He attached a picture of Kishi to the paper and sat back to look at his efforts. Not too bad, he thought. He just hoped someone would come across her and help. He had spent a sleepless night listening for a bark or a whine. Once or twice he was sure he had heard something and had leapt out of bed with relief, flinging open the door crying:

"Kishi!"

But there had been no dog there.

Only the lonely howl of the wind and a flurry of snow.

With a heavy heart, Halvor set out towards the town with his home-made poster, a hammer and some nails. There was a notice board just outside an old inn. He would put it up there, where the other hunters would see it as they went for their warming ale. He could ask around as well. Someone must know something.

In the distance, Halvor saw a troll-woman hurrying against the cold. She kept her head down and was wearing a worn, red scarf tied under the chin. Her simple shift and shawl were no protection in this weather, and she had nothing on her hairy feet. As he approached, he could see she had a rolled-up picture under her arm.

"Hey – you!" he called to her.

The troll stopped in her tracks and looked startled.

"Don't worry, Mrs Troll," Halvor reassured her. "I won't harm you."

Hildi was uncertain. She was very wary of the Big People. She had taken one of her beautiful forest pictures to trade with at her usual shop, but had not been successful. The Big Woman had shooed her out saying there was nothing for her today and people wanted food in the town, not worthless pictures. They had been harsh words and they stung Hildi more than the cruel wind which she battled against on her way home. All she had needed were some glass bottles for her honey medicines, but no luck. Now, she just wanted to get back to Thom and their cosy dwelling in the forest away from the town.

Halvor touched her arm and showed Hildi the poster and picture he had. She stepped to one side, out of view of the houses and shops.

"You live in the forest, Mrs Troll. I have lost my dog. Have you seen her? She is called –" Halvor swallowed, "Kishi." Somehow it was hard to say his faithful friend's name. There was a lump which ached in his throat.

Hildi was not keen to hang around. She knew that other Big People were not friendly towards trolls, and she didn't want to stop on this road where she was exposed.

"Nay, nay," she said shaking her head, forgetting to avoid troll-talk, "nay doggor in foresh." She pulled her shawl more closely around her and made as if to leave.

"Please!" implored Halvor. "Look out for her, will you? She has a blue collar. My name is Halvor. I live in this town – everyone knows me – send a message if you can."

Hildi looked into the Big Man's eyes. She could see his anguish and it touched her heart. She nodded quickly and, looking around her to check she had not been seen, stepped out again on to the road home.

"Don't forget, Mrs Troll, will you?" Halvor called after her. "Please!"

~~~

Dotta decided to have another go at the special sleeping potion. The last had burnt at the bottom of her fire-pot as she had struggled with Grimhildr to extinguish the flames on her apron ties. The goats had been milked, the animals had been tended and fed, and her latest cheese had been turned in its bath of brine ready for stacking in the cold shelter. The bats slept.

Grimhildr had disappeared into the forest, warmly wrapped in the goat-hair blanket from her bed. She took strong troll-strides along the paths which were so familiar to her kind. If there *was* a missing dog, as Pipi and Fug had said, it would probably be near a troll-path rather than the Big

People's tracks. The Big Man would have found it otherwise. She took her hickory walking stick with her to aid her along the way and to poke gently into the frozen winter bushes, which were sharp and prickly to touch. She knew the chances of finding the dog alive, after a night as bitter as they had just had, were slim.

Dotta mixed equal portions of honey and liquorice root-base as before. As she stirred, she screwed her wrinkly face up and thought hard. Now what else had she used yesterday? It had been such a wonderful, dreamy fragrance! What was it? She shuffled over to her herb cupboard and looked in. Fennel? Dried raspberry leaf? Winter mountain-rose petals? Dandelion?

Umm...

Dandelion leaves seemed to ring a bell.

Dotta shook her head in confusion. It was so hard to remember all the different combinations she had tried recently. She knew that Grimhildr was right when she had told Dotta to keep a record of the ingredients. For a while she had done just that, using a piece of charcoal from the fireside and an old piece of slate, drawing pictures of the herbs used with simple counting strokes to indicate the amounts. Then Dotta had run out of slate, and the one she had used got cracked and split when an over-exuberant, recovered fox had decided to chase a young hare across the floor of the shack. She really must ask Hairy Bogley, the Collector, to find her something to use instead, she thought. Perhaps he could make a night-time trip to the Big People and bogle some paper for her! That would be a real treat! What luxury!

For now, though, Dotta had to concentrate and try to remember. In went the dried dandelion leaves. Was that the same amount? She shook in some more just to make sure and returned to the herb cupboard. Lime flower stems? No. She shook her head again. They were too rare. She wouldn't have used those. As the little troll returned the stems to the shelf, her hairy hand brushed against the chamomile and her face suddenly shone. Of course! In it went, with some extra for good measure, and the fire-pot was stirred with her great wooden spoon.

Hmm, hmm.

Bubble and cool.

This time, she was going to watch the potion carefully and keep her apron tied securely.

Hmm, hmm.

Bubble and cool.

A knock at the old pine door made Dotta look up.

"Halloo?" she called.

"Halloo, Dotta! Es meer, Hildi!" a familiar voice answered. Dotta wiped her sticky hands on her splashed apron and went to let her dear sister-troll in. They greeted each other, holding hands and bending so their foreheads touched in traditional troll manner, before throwing their arms around each other and kissing warmly. Tracker, Hildi's dog, rushed in, all frosty fur and lolloping licks.

"Gooshty morgy, Hildi! Comli in homerig en drinkoosh tay! Es freezorig outen, brrrrrrr!"

Dotta pushed her rocking chair nearer to the fire and beckoned Hildi towards it. Hildi nodded and thanked her sister, putting down her basket of smoked fish and honey collected at the end of that summer from Thom's hives. The trolls had been wise enough to read nature's signs that year and were well-prepared for the harsh winter months. The summer's bees had been busy and Thom had collected their honeyed sweetness regularly to store for later. He had made many fishing trips in Mistig Vorter when the autumn berries were abundant, gathering fish in his beautifully-crafted nets and smoking them over the fire in the cradle that Grimhildr had made. As a consequence, the trolls could look after each other now and they busily swapped honey and fish for goat's cheese and yogurt, chattering all the while.

Hildi's two mice, Tailo and Scratchen, had come along for the ride, as they often did, in Hildi's basket. As soon as they could, they clambered out and scampered across the kitchen floor in search of crumbs and fallen cheese bits. This was always their favourite trip. Dotta's kitchen floor always had all manner of tasty morsels.

It was just as Hildi was telling her sister about the meeting with Halvor that they heard a sudden, furious bubbling, followed by a huge **splosh!** and a

sizzzzzle!

Dotta turned to the fire and threw up her hands in horror. A volcano was erupting over the sides of the fire-pot!

"LAVA! LAVA ATTACK!" squawked Tailo, as he tried to follow Scratchen who had dashed up the nearest wall to get off the floor. As usual, Tailo's fat tummy prevented him and he did nothing but bounce around the kitchen shrieking and squeaking. Tracker barked in fright and made for cover under the table.

Dotta looked beseechingly at Hildi. Where was Grimhildr when she needed her?

~~~

The trip wire and noose had been cunningly hidden. Grimhildr scowled when she saw the cruel trap. How many times had she seen this now? How many animals had she rescued from the biting snare? How many more would there be?

"Biggy Menor catchen animores!" she growled, bashing at the deer trap with her gnarled stick. It snapped shut around the hickory and Grimhildr had to twist hard to release its grip. "Stoofid, dedden Biggy Menor!"

She was just about to stomp further into the depths of the forest when she heard a weak whimper, almost indiscernible, but definitely there. She bent down to peer through the stiff bracken.

Two chocolate-brown eyes peered back.

~~~

The fire-pot had been rescued from over the fire and was left to cool in a corner of the shack whilst Hildi and Dotta scrubbed the hearth, on their hands and knees. The burnt, sticky liquid had set hard and took some shifting.

"Oh Dotta!" laughed Hildi, sitting back on her hairy heels for a moment's rest. "U dreamoori!"

Dotta smiled sheepishly at her sister and wiped her brow with the back of a sticky hand, leaving a smear across her forehead. "Oor littelor secresht, Hildi!" she replied, putting one finger to her lips.

Tailo had found the fire-pot. His greedy eyes lit up as he saw the trickled caramel goo which ran down the side.

"Oh boy, oh boy!" he cried in ecstasy. "Let me at it!" and he proceeded to chomp the brown, honeyed stickiness with his yellow teeth. Scratchen was more cautious. He didn't trust Dotta's brews at the best of times, and this certainly wasn't one to test. He watched his mouse-mate scoffing and waited for the inevitable.

"Mmmuff, mmmuff!" Tailo tried to speak but, oddly, couldn't get his teeth to unstick. He looked to Scratchen in rising panic. "Mmmuff, mmmuff!" he repeated, pointing with a mousey paw to his clamped mouth.

"Hmm?" replied Scratchen, pretending to inspect his claws. "Are you trying to tell me something? Hmm?"

Tailo breathed heavily through his tiny, twitchy nose. This was no time for playing around. He might never get his mouth open again! How would he eat then?

It was just as Hildi saw him turning a rather odd shade of blue and had rushed to plunge his face under some running water, that the door of the shack was flung open. A shivering, goose-pimpling wind wrapped itself around their ankles announcing Grimhildr's arrival.

In her arms, stiff with cold and barely breathing, was a bundle of dog. She was wrapped in Grimhildr's blanket but one paw hung out, lifelessly. The blood was frozen into the fur. Her eyes were closed.

Into the depths ~

Close by his mother's side, the young minke calf strengthened and learnt to ride the currents of the ocean. His pointed snout continually turned to her for signs and encouragement as they powered through the fathoms, twice-blowing, arching and diving. She pushed him harder and harder to plunge deeper and for longer, keeping flukes in the icy water and thrusting down with a cascading rush. The pale cream of his underbelly flashed against the deepening grey of his back as he twisted through the waters, changing direction and speed.

Five short months had passed since the minke's birth, and now he was learning to sieve through the sea-soup for polar plankton and krill, even chasing schools of sardines, anchovies and herring; ploughing icily northwards, unaware of the danger awaiting them.

Chapter Three

*F*lutter-flutter, flitt-flatt!

Pipi and Fug flitted through the dusk of late afternoon, strong wings beating, as they followed the echoes of their high-pitched clicks and calls. They swooped expertly through the pine trees of the forest towards the town, Pipi leading as always. They usually played bat games of hide-and-seek just here, in the gathering gloom on the edge of the trees, each searching the other and giving high speed chases to out-fly them. Or they would, on warmer evenings, dive and lunge at tiny flying insects which massed in swarms of tasty chewiness. Or they would hang and swing, and swing and hang, just to pass some time, thinking about batty things.

But not now.

Now they didn't have time for games, or gnat-nibbling, or idling away a few moments in bat-thought.

In their time at Dotta and Grimhildr's, they had seen animals come and go. They had seen how the patient care of the trolls had revived flagging bodies and enthused exhausted minds. They had seen old, young, wounded, sick, starving and thirsty animals pick up their appetites and their spirits with the love shown to them, leaving the little shack in the forest revitalised and happy once more.

But this one was different.

This one was a very sick case.

And it could involve a Big Person.

Pipi and Fug had been dispatched to the town to find the poster of which Hildi had spoken. It was essential to identify the broken dog which had been found deep in the forest, before contacting her owner. If this was *not* Halvor's dog, there would be no point in leading a Big Man to troll homes. They had to be kept secret as much as possible. If this *was* Halvor's dog however, he should be told. Hildi was sure of the pain in his eyes when he had spoken to her in the biting wind earlier that day. She knew devotion when she saw it. They would have to relieve his distress and reunite man with dog if they could.

Squeaking shrilly to each other, the flaggermusses made speedy progress towards the buildings of the Big People. They knew the region like the back of their wings. Their flying area was large, over forest, fjord and town. There were no obstacles which they could not swoop to avoid, and they could cover distances rapidly; they were always together, synchronised acrobats.

The poster was already looking tatty. The weather had caused it to rip from one nail, and the corner hung damp and forlorn. Pipi and Fug hung upside-down on the notice board to catch their breath. They squinted down at the picture.

"Why is the dog standing on her head?" wondered Fug.

"Dogs will do anything for a treat," replied Pipi.

~~~

Dotta knelt by the trembling dog all through the night. At first, there was grave doubt that the animal would survive her injuries from the cruel trap, and then even more concern that she would not recover from the extreme cold of the forest floor where she had been lying. Her wounded leg had been washed in salt water and then tenderly dressed with honey ointment and clean bandaging. The cuts were deep slashes because the dog had struggled to free herself, but now they were bound comfortably and the honey soothed the intense pain to a heart-beat throb. Dotta had used the warmer goat-hair blanket from the bed to wrap around her patient and, every hour, she edged the frozen dog a little closer to the fire so that the warmth grew slowly and gently. As dusk became night, and night became the darkest of deepest black, the little dog struggled to waken. As she twitched and whimpered, Dotta laid a soothing troll hand on the brown fur of her neck and stroked, softly humming ancient troll tunes. She loosened the blue collar, wonderingly.

Was this the dog Hildi had spoken of?

Would the little bats be able to find the proof?

Would it be safe to tell the Big Man?

Dotta's tired little head dropped and her eyelids began to close. Grimhildr snored gently in the rocking chair close by. All the other animals slept soundly as time slowly ticked its way through the long, dark hours. The brown dog fought to survive, tortured by dreams of snares and biting metal teeth, still feeling the desolation of being lost in the forest.

It was just as a thin, cold light began to break under the door, that there was a familiar scritch-scratch at the window. Dotta awoke with a start and tried to get to her hairy feet. Her knees, though, were locked in a cramp and made her suddenly stumble and shout out.

"Grimhildr! Mi littelor leggors hurtig so badli! Helpen meer, pleasor!"

Her sister snorted awake and grabbed her hickory stick. She passed it to Dotta and heaved her up on a strong arm.

"Nay worrish, Dotta," Grimhildr reassured her. "Im strongish foor oos tvo!"

The scritch-scratching at the window became more frantic and then the two trolls realised what had woken them. Two flaggermuss noses were pressed against the glass, a piece of paper spread out between their two mouths.

"Pipi en Fug!" Dotta exclaimed, rubbing her sore knees, trying to get some life back into her little, hairy troll legs. Grimhildr let the bats in. They fluttered to the floor with part of Halvor's poster hanging soggily between them.

"Thanken, mi dearigs, thanken," Dotta said, straightening up at last. She and Grimhildr picked up the piece of poster together with the attached picture, and smoothed them out on the sturdy tabletop. Both pored over the small section of writing, but made little sense of it. The picture, however, was quite clear. Although the happy dog with bright eyes, ears cocked and head on one side bore little resemblance to the sad scrap lying in front of the fire, the markings on the fur and the blue of the collar were identical. The trolls remembered Hildi's visit. The Big Man had called his dog Kishi. And he had been Halvor.

"Kishi?" Dotta whispered to the forlorn bundle of fur wrapped in a blanket. "Kishi?"

One brown ear flicked and the dog whined softly. Grimhildr joined Dotta at the animal's side and stroked her gently.

"Kishi doggor? Varken oop mi lovelor," Dotta continued to whisper. There was another flick of an ear and the merest hint of a tail-wag. Ever so slowly, two chocolate-brown eyes opened and Kishi looked into the concerned faces of the trolls.

"Halloo, Kishi. Gooshty doggor! U shtay bi fior, Kishi, en restig. U in Grimhildr en Hildi's homerig. Ve helpen hurtig animores." These reassuring words, spoken in soothing tones, made Kishi relax. She accepted a small drink of water gratefully, and cautiously stretched her bad leg out in front of her. A deep ache made her growl. She licked around the bandaging and adjusted her position so she was more comfortable.

Dotta was elated. It had been a long night.

~~~

The collar was heavy to fly with. It proved too difficult for Pipi and Fug to carry between them and so they took it in turns to loop it, hanging over their tiny necks, and transported it as best they could. The weight made them fly lower than usual and this caused problems, because there were many extra obstacles to avoid. As the carrier became too tired, the other bat would take over by swooping underneath and looping through the collar, both flying in tandem for a short distance, until the transfer from one to the other was complete. In addition to this, the bats were sleepy. They had already struggled with the poster and picture, flying through the night. Then, after what seemed like a very short rest around breakfast time, they had been given further instructions. Ideally, they would have preferred to have been tucked upside-down at this time of day, bat-dreaming, but that was not to be.

Dotta and Grimhildr had consulted with Hildi and Thom as to the best possible plan. All were certain that the injured dog was Kishi, and all were equally certain that Halvor should be told. Big People, however, did not understand bat-speak and so the only way to let Halvor know that Kishi had been found would be to take the collar as proof. None of the trolls wanted to go into the town and find the Big Man themselves. Pipi and Fug were to find the right house, show Halvor the collar, and get him to follow them back to the forest. The real risk was that, because Kishi was not well enough to move yet, Halvor would have to be led to the little shack, once so hidden amongst the trees.

It would not be hidden any longer.

"Oor homerig nics secresht in foresh," Grimhildr had warned the others. "Dedden Biggy Menor comli en catchen dee trolls!"

The others had nodded in understanding and they had tried to think of other options. However, nobody could come up with a different idea. Dotta had listened to all this with growing concern. She looked at the pretty brown dog and couldn't contain herself any longer.

"Nay worrish!" she blurted out suddenly. "Kishi shtay wit oos! Biggy Menor nics comli!" The other trolls looked at her pleading face and shook their hairy heads.

"Nay, Dotta," Hildi replied, putting a sisterly arm around her. "Kishi es Halvor's doggor." Dotta's weather-worn face crumpled and a hot tear rolled down to her chin.

"Kishi nics foor meer? Kishi nics shtay wit Dotta?"

"Nay, Dotta," they all said as one. Whatever the risk to themselves, they must do the right thing and tell Halvor of Kishi's whereabouts. Dotta would have to let another of her beloved animals go back to its proper home. The little flaggermusses had then been sent to the town with the bluebell collar, despite their yearning for a good rest.

~~~

Halvor ate the last stale crust of bread from his cupboard and wondered if he would ever see his loyal dog again. The bread turned over and over in his mouth as he chewed, but he didn't seem able to swallow it. His empty stomach grumbled for food, yet he had no appetite. He sat in his cold house and had never felt so alone. The fire had long since gone out and he had not the heart to rekindle the flames. He was full of remorse.

How could he have lost Kishi?

Why did he send her off on her own?

What would he do without her?

With a heavy sigh, Halvor got to his feet and decided to crunch along the bleak, snow-filled road to the inn. He could check his poster, perhaps call in for a jug of warm ale and ask after Kishi again. Better than sitting here on his own, in silence. His great boots were unyielding and stiff, not soft and warm as they should have been, had they been by the fire. His gloves were still wet from the last search through the forest, his hat frosty, and his scarf gave little comfort.

As he took long strides, Halvor strained his eyes to see the notice board, a little further down the road. Two black dots seemed to be making swooping circles, swirling in front of him. He shook his head to clear them. Obviously, he was so tired his eyes were not seeing clearly. The closer he got, the more the dots circled and he felt drawn towards them, trance-like. Now, he saw two dots and a small blue ring circling and swooping. Just the same blue as his dear Kishi's collar, Halvor thought sadly to himself and blinked hard to focus better. He peered ahead.

Not two dots at all. Two bats!

The Big Man raised his gloved fists and rubbed his tired eyes. Bats? In the daytime? It made no sense. And then he saw the collar. Without doubt, it was Kishi's collar swinging from bat-to-bat as they flitted around the notice board. Then, as he struggled to hurry towards them, the collar dropped and fell with a soft flumph into the snow.

"You dropped it!" squeaked Pipi to Fug.

"You didn't pass it properly!" Fug piped back.

"You should have swooped better!"

"You should have held on longer!"

"How do we pick it up now?"

But the little bats needn't have worried. Halvor arrived panting and red-faced, dived into the snow, grabbed the collar and held it up high in delight.

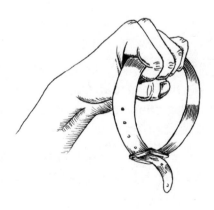

"My Kishi's collar! Kishi, where are you? Are you here?" The Big Man's voice boomed and filled the air as he looked around him wildly.

"Looks like we found the right one!" Pipi called to Fug. "Seems to be the Halvor chap we need! Pretty clever, eh?"

The two bats flew to each other and slapped wings in self-congratulation. "Now to get him to come back with us!"

Halvor fingered the collar fondly and looked around him. There was no sign of anyone – man or dog. Just two crazy bats, out in the daytime and apparently intent on flying around his head. He couldn't really believe they had been flying with the collar, but where else had it come from? It couldn't have just dropped into the snow from nowhere.

Pipi flew onto Halvor's shoulder and tugged at the peak of his hat. He gave a start and tried to flick her away. Pipi was not going to give up. With a determined yank, the hat came off Halvor's head and, gripping it tightly in her tiny feet, the bat swooped it away into the sky.

"Hey! My hat! You, bat! Come back!" flustered Halvor, flapping his arms madly. "Hey! A hat's got my bat – I mean a bat's got my hat!"

Pipi curled in on a tight turn and plunged towards the Big Man. He lunged at the hat trying to grab it, but the little bat was far too quick. Within seconds, she was away again and flew with speed to Fug. The hat was passed between them and they returned, time and time again, to Halvor.

"Give me my bat, you mad hat!" he panted, thoroughly confused, leaping and snatching at the air which rushed past him, to no avail. Pipi looked over to Fug who was lining up for another dive.

"Fug!" she shrilled. "Lead him away – I'll catch up!"

Fug needed no further instruction. As always, the bats worked in perfect harmony. Fug flew ahead, just slowing enough for Halvor to catch up a little, then Pipi darted over his head, or between his legs, or around the side to take over when the hat became too heavy. They ducked and dived and swirled and swept their way from the town with Halvor in hot pursuit, Kishi's collar firmly gripped in his hand.

Towards the forest.

Further and further from the town. Along the hidden troll paths and the ways of the fae creatures.

Bringing this Big Man closer and closer.

Nearer and nearer.

To the home of the trolls.

~~~

A net of ice ~

The warmer waters of the minke's birth were left far behind and the ocean depths were now much colder, darker and less welcoming. Following the grunts and thuds of his mother, replying with raspy sounds of his own, the two made their way north towards distant arctic regions in search of fish. The weather above the surface had worsened; the sky was now a dark purple and continually threw hail which spattered the swell of the water with stinging orbs of ice.

For a short while they had swum with two other minkes, and even shadowed a lone fishing vessel, breaching alongside, but knew they had more chance of food if they were just two. Mother kept careful watch of her young calf, encouraging and teaching, proud of his developing strength.

Without warning though, there was a change in the water. As the whales rose to the surface, it became more difficult to turn and twist. Slushy crystals clouded their view and felt gritty in their mouths. The mother hesitated and sounded a note of instruction to her son.

She attempted to turn around, to return along the swimming route they had just travelled.

A frozen block prevented her.

She twisted to turn in the other direction. The slush dragged against her body, slowing her. She pushed her way round, grunting with effort, and began to move her tail flukes downwards ready to escape – but she could not raise them.

The loving mother knew a sudden panic.

A feverish second of realisation.

She was trapped in a pocket of water within pack ice. There was nowhere to turn. No way forward. No way back.

The young minke discovered he was locked out of her ice cage. He thrashed about, trying to break through, with no success. The ice was impenetrable.

He was left with no choice. He had to turn south.

Alone.

Chapter Four

"*H*at, bat! Bat, hat!"

A sudden noise made Dotta look up.

Had it been a shout?

The wolverine she was nursing stopped sucking. He grabbed the bottle teat between his sharp teeth and growled, long and low. The hair on the back of his neck pricked up and his lips formed their first ever fierce snarl. Dotta dropped him to the floor in alarm. The partridge fluttered to a sheltered corner and hid her head under her good wing. If she couldn't see anything, then perhaps she herself would not be seen. The mountain goats outside began to blart and huddle together; a warning of danger.

Dotta was alone. Grimhildr had gone to destroy the trap which had caught Kishi. Hildi and Thom had returned to their own home to feed mice, Grimo their cat, and Tracker. There was nobody to help.

A sudden fluttering at the window caught Dotta's eye. A navy-blue peaked cap was flapping against the glass. A hat without a head? How very odd! Then a flaggermuss face thrust itself forward, amidst earnest squeakings and chirrups. The bats were back – but they looked frantic. Whatever was going on?

It was just as the nervous little troll was going to open the window that she heard heavy boot-thuds approaching. Once more the wolverine growled, crouched low, and he raised his hackles further. The goats became even more agitated and set up a real commotion outside the shack.

Blim! Blam! Blim! Blam!

The old door shook with four deafening blows and Dotta cried out in fright. She clutched her old shawl around her and stood frozen to the spot.

Blam! Blim! Blam! Blim!

The thumps came again and then a booming voice:

"Hello! Open the door! Please!"

Dotta had no choice but to reply. The door would be knocked off its hinges if she didn't. Without thinking, she called out in troll-talk.

"Yo, yo! Im comli!"

She glanced quickly around the kitchen at the animals. The wolverine stayed at her ankles, guarding. All the others had hidden in boxes and baskets and corners, and under the beds. Kishi, however, was different. She was not afraid. She looked suddenly alert and bright. She was attempting to get to her feet for the first time, whining and beginning to wag her tail.

"Kishi?" Dotta questioned. This could mean only one thing. The bats had successfully found Halvor and brought him to their home in the forest. This was both good and bad. Good, because that *had* been their plan and it *was* right that Kishi should be reunited with her master. Bad, because Dotta was on her own and was told *never* to open the door to someone she didn't know.

The Big Man called again. This time he was quieter, having heard Dotta's tremulous voice in answer to his shouting. "I won't harm you! I just want to know if you have my Kishi! Some mad bats brought her collar to me and then stole my hat. I'm sure they intended to lead me here. Please open the door so we can talk! I won't even come in."

The wolverine shuffled low, down to the door well and sniffed suspiciously. Dotta knew he would guard her well, young though he was, but she still had to be careful.

"Hab u dedden gunnig?" she asked sternly, her face close to a crack, trying to peer out.

"What?" came the reply. "I mean, pardon?"

"Hab u dedden gunnig?" Dotta repeated.

"I don't understand you, Mrs Troll!"

Dotta shook her head and realised her mistake.

"Have you got a gun?" Dotta asked once more. "We trolls don't trust guns, or people who have them!" She flushed with excitement. How proud Grimhildr would be of her; speaking out so strongly and not being dotty for once!

"No, of course not," Halvor said more quietly. "I said I mean you no harm. Do you have my little pet?"

At the sound of his gentler tone, the growling at Dotta's ankles calmed and she reached out a trembling hand to open the door.

Slowly… slowly.

Creak… creak.

And there he stood. The Big Man.

Dotta stared straight at Halvor's leather-belted waist. Her eyes travelled slowly upwards, past his coat buttons to his broad shoulders and up to his shaggy beard. There were little droplets on it which seemed to be frozen, and his breath could be seen as a panting fog. The nipping, icy wind had made his nose red, and his anxious eyes were stinging and watery.

...And there he stood. The Big Man...

"Please, Mrs Troll," he implored. "Tell me you have her!"

Dotta then saw the same anguish that Hildi had described and she forgot her fear. Her soft heart melted at the sight of someone who needed her help. She relaxed her wrinkled frown and smiled. It was as though the sun had come out.

"Yes," she said quietly. "We have your Kishi. You must come in and warm yourself."

~~~

By the time Grimhildr returned, Dotta had set out a feast of smoked fish, herby cheese, rye bread and goats' milk. A jar of Hildi's best heather honey was in the middle of the table, and water was boiling over the fire ready to make nettle tea. Halvor was sitting on the floor with his precious Kishi on his lap, and his great arms were wrapped around her. The other animals had relaxed and were in their usual places; sleeping, playing or licking their wounds. Grimhildr hesitated at the door for a moment, to take the situation in. All seemed calm and her sister greeted her with a sad smile.

"Halvor hab Kishi," Dotta said, quietly.

"Yo, yo," replied Grimhildr with a nod. "So, so."

Another loved one to leave. The young wolverine was thriving and soon he would have to be taught to live wild in the mountains. The spring would soon be here and, without doubt, he would be ready. The two old badgers had left the shack today, still limping slightly, but happy to find their sett waiting. They had scuffled down into the ground without a backward glance, relieved to be back in their earthy home. Dotta planned to remove the splint from the grey partridge later so that she could test her wing and learn to fly once more, hopefully avoiding danger from now on. So many animal friends had passed their way, but never stayed. And now, pretty Kishi would soon be gone. Sometimes it was hard to love as much as Dotta did.

Halvor stood up when Grimhildr entered. The little room suddenly shrank and became less light. He reached out for her hairy troll-hand and pumped her arm up and down.

"I believe it was you who found my Kishi!" he exclaimed. "Thank you a million times. You cannot possibly know what this means to me!"

"She would not have been hurt if Big Men left the forest creatures alone," Grimhildr answered darkly, but she nodded at Halvor and took her seat at the table, keeping a wary eye on him. "There should be no need for you to hunt in the forest, or for others to set snares. You come from the town where they catch fish; you can trade with other Big People. There is no need to trespass where we live."

Dotta was concerned. She had spent longer in Halvor's presence and she knew him to be a good man. She did not want Grimhildr to be unfriendly towards him.

"Nay, Grimhildr," she intervened. "Halvor es gooshty! Halvor es hungeror en dursty. Comli en eatig, pleasor!"

Halvor joined them at the table and fell upon the food with gusto. He hadn't eaten properly for days and the trolls' food tasted wonderful. The goats' cheese had been warmed by the fire and oozed onto the bread in a rich squelch. Just the smell of the smoked fish made Halvor's mouth water and he gulped the creamy milk, not caring that it ran down his beard a little. The two trolls glanced at each other when they saw his hunger. They had never seen such an appetite – or food disappear so rapidly from their table!

When, at last, Halvor had eaten his fill, he wiped his milky beard with the back of his hand and pushed back his chair. He looked at the empty plates, the sea of crumbs and fish bones, and then across at the bemused faces of his hosts.

"Oh, I'm sorry!" he blurted out in sudden embarrassment. "I was starving! It was so delicious! I have never tasted food as good as that! The honey must have come from faeries!"

"Just Thom's happy bees," replied Dotta, smiling. "Surely you have honey like that in the town?"

"Not at all! We have *never* had honey as sweet as that," the Big Man replied, shaking his head, his face clouding over suddenly. He paused. "Just now, there is very little of *anything* to eat, actually."

Dotta reached for the boiling water and poured it on to dried nettle leaves in a large pot. She poked at them with a rough wooden spoon until the liquid brewed a deep green. Kishi lay at her master's feet, head resting on her good paw, the other leg stretched out in front of her. She slept peacefully, with no agitated whimperings or feelings of being lost. Man and dog were obviously meant to be together.

"Is it the bad winter which has made the difference?" Grimhildr asked Halvor.

"It is very bad," he replied and his beard seemed to sag as he spoke. "That is why I was hunting, you see. The boats have not been out for a few weeks now. The fish stocks we stored up are gone. Trading with other towns is difficult because transport is affected and we have no fish to sell. Few people have money, and any food that is available is very expensive."

"So the Big People go into the forest to hunt and set snares," Grimhildr added, frowning.

"We have no choice. The people are getting more and more desperate. The men can't fish and the women need them to be working so they can sell."

The trolls looked around their little home. How fortunate they were! Their way of life was largely self-sufficient. They had all they needed from the goats, and by careful storage of food through the summer months when it was plentiful. They looked after each other's needs and didn't have to make money. The smoked fish lasted through the winter, the cheeses were kept carefully in the cold shed, Thom's honey nourished them, and the dried herbs kept them well and meant they could have soups and tea. They had fresh milk and yogurt. Their homes were warmed with crackling fires from gathered kindling and fallen trees. What more could they need?

"How have you managed before in harsh winters?" Dotta questioned, bringing the steaming tea to the table. "This isn't the first time it has been so cold or the sea beyond the fjord so rough."

"We were always fine until the ban…"

"The ban?" the trolls chorused.

Halvor hesitated. He hardly dared bring the subject up. He looked around the animal lovers' home and then rubbed his mouth as if to rid himself of the words he had just spoken.

"What ban?" prompted Grimhildr, fixing the Big Man with a hard stare.

Halvor swallowed. "Nothing. No. It doesn't matter. I was speaking without thinking. Forget it."

Dotta was suddenly confused. She had spent some time being sensible and brave and strong now, and was running out of steam a bit. Grimhildr had a stern look on her face and Dotta didn't like it. Also, talking to Big People was tiring as she had to concentrate on her words, and now she felt decidedly dozy.

"Gooshty!" she smiled with some relief. "We'll forget it then. More tay?"

"Nay, Dotta!" Grimhildr barked, a little too sharply. "Nay!" and turning once more to Halvor, repeated her question. "What ban?"

Halvor cleared his throat. It was *his* turn to feel nervous now. He did not want to upset these gentle troll-people, especially when they had been so kind. There was no avoiding the subject though. Grimhildr would not let the matter drop. It was as though she had guessed what the Big Man had been about to say.

"The whale ban!" he choked out at last. "We used to be allowed to harvest whales, but now we have a ban in our waters! We have to watch the numbers."

"*Harvest* whales?" Grimhildr almost spat the words. "Don't you mean **kill** them?"

"Nay, Grimhildr! Nay! Shtop!" cried Dotta in anguish, unable to believe what she had just heard. She was getting so agitated, she was unable to follow the conversation properly and her tired old eyes began to fill with tears. "Walloos es speshy animores! Nay! Im so sadli!"

Halvor looked crestfallen. He tried to explain as best he could. "Yes, I'm afraid you are right. It has been our custom for many years in this area. Men in huge boats used to go out to the deepest parts of the ocean in search of whales. Minkes usually, in this area. Stinke minkes as we call them!"

The trolls were horrified. Grimhildr's suspicions were correct.

"But why?"

"Stinkes? Because they eat so much fish their breath smells when you get close up to them. Also, they are good at diving just when we want them to break the surface, which is tricky of them…"

"I *mean*, why do you want to *kill* them?" Grimhildr persisted. Dotta was speechless.

"For food," came the reply. "The meat and blubber are eaten in traditional dishes in our area."

Dotta began to look and feel rather sick.

"And to sell on to others to make money so we can buy the things we need…" Halvor's voice trailed off as he saw the look on the trolls' faces.

"Hang your head in shame, Big Man!" Grimhildr growled. "Money again! With you Big People it's **always** about money!"

"Please understand!" Halvor continued hastily, "I have never done it myself!" His voice lowered. "But I know men who have. The whole town has relied upon minke hunting for ages, and now times are hard. We are starving."

An awkward silence followed.

Dotta decided to clear the table. Hopefully this would help to clear the air.

~~~

Much later, when fond farewells had been exchanged between Kishi and the trolls, Halvor had left. He had given them his most grateful thanks and promised to be a true friend to them should they ever be in need. His humble words lingered in the evening air.

"I am in your debt," he had told them. "I can never repay you for your kindness and skill in caring for Kishi."

The bats had woken as the cold dusk fell and after a few tit-bits from Dotta's hand, they had left for a night flutter. Dotta hoped they might find some new ingredients for her special sleeping potion so she could spend a few happy hours experimenting in the morning.

They didn't.

Pipi and Fug came across a great clamour of excitement in the town.

At the harbour's edge.

~~~

Towards danger ~

Following instinct, the young minke made his way south, alone for the first time in his short life, and confused. No longer had he a mother to guide him. No protection. No feeling of belonging. The ocean waters seemed less inviting to him now. He had lost the thrill of discovering new depths; he was concerned only with finding food and surviving. He felt that if he could travel back to his birth waters, he would regain some of the safety he had known. He hoped that perhaps he would meet other whales like himself, and they would swim together.

The emptiness stretched ahead of him.

Occasionally his spirits were lifted by a shoal of herrings or the odd squid, but he was not well-practised at seizing the moment and many evaded capture. Some krill could be sifted through the water, which kept him going; his travels became a constant search for food.

Gradually, the extreme cold of his surroundings lessened. The minke knew he was in a more southerly region. The furious pounding of waves had ceased. When he broke into the air, to breathe through his twin blowholes, the surface was calmer. The water was shallower and welcomed him into the inlet.

Beckoned him.

Lured him in.

Wrapped itself around him and whispered to him that he was safe.

The little whale felt relieved of his anxiety. He relaxed, breaching at leisure, dipping in and out almost in play…

…unaware that the twinkling lantern lights of the Big People were laughing at his innocence.

Chapter Five

*P*eep! Peep! Toowip! Tooweep!

Dotta was playing haunting mountain troll-music on her pipes. She kept them in a small wooden box underneath her bed and found they helped whenever she wanted to soothe herself, or the animals in her care. As fresh snow fell outside the trolls' shack, covering Halvor's footprints, it felt as if every last trace of Kishi was disappearing with them. The notes rose and fell, dancing in the air, swirling and looping-the-loop. They spiralled out into the night, mingling with the wood smoke from the fire, floating through the branches of forest pines, down towards the town. On a very still night, the Big People sometimes thought they could hear the faint tinkle of far-away melodies, but it was so soft that they often just turned in their beds and fell deeper into sleep.

Tonight, however, no-one would hear Dotta.

Tonight, there was too much noise at the harbour's edge.

Tonight, the Big People gathered with torches and lanterns, shouting and pointing, pushing and shoving, all trying to get a clearer view of the dark water which stretched before them to the open sea.

...gathered with torches and lanterns...

Pipi and Fug flitted and swooped overhead. They, too, were searching the water to see what all the fuss might be about. They knew they should be looking for other ingredients for Dotta's special sleeping potion, and checking on Kishi through Halvor's windows, but all that would have to wait. This was far more important.

Suddenly, a great roar came from the crowd and, as one, they seethed forward even closer to the edge, arms waving and fingers pointing.

"There! Did you see it?" one Big Man bellowed to his companion. "Over there! In the water!"

"A pikehead!"

"A little finner!"

All seemed to yell, cry out, scream and screech at once. Hungry desperation and wild excitement drove them to push closer to the protective sea wall, so some were crushed up against it, flailing their arms, needing space.

"A STINKY MINKE!" the Big People bawled. "GET HIM!"

The bats dived over the heads of the gathered mob and skimmed the surface of the inky wetness, their high-pitched squeaks only audible to each other. A white flipper patch, clearly diamond-shaped, broke the surface for an instant and then slipped out of sight. Gone.

Safe for the time being in the depths.

Hidden from view in the darkness.

Only reflections of light glinted and danced in the eager, greedy eyes of the onlookers.

Halvor looked up when he heard the shouts from the harbour. Kishi had slept soundly at the foot of his bed since returning home and now, thanks to the nourishing food the trolls had given her, together with the loving care she needed, she was a new dog.

"Something's happening out there, Kishi," Halvor murmured, playing with her velvety ears. "I'm not sure it sounds good."

Kishi gave her paw a quick lick and jumped down to scratch at the door.

"No, little dog, not tonight," her master replied to her whining. "The night is cold and we must stay here. Tomorrow we will see what all the fuss was about."

~~~

Dotta had an idea. The morning had brought it to her like a flash of sunshine. The special sleeping potion was so *nearly* right. She had remembered the dreamy effects it had on her as she had stirred and brewed it before. Now, with a dash of one final ingredient, she might just have the full effect she was searching for. And she had thought of the very thing. If it did work, and gently put animals into a dreamy slumber, she could do so much more to help them when in pain. If she got the dose right, they would awaken feeling relaxed and calm, with healing already under way. Dotta felt a tingle of excitement and the first rush of happiness since Kishi had left. This might just be the answer! She must tend to the animals and then wrap up warmly to visit Hildi. Hildi was sure to have just what she needed.

It was just as she was removing her sticky, spattered apron to hang on the hook by the door, that Pipi and Fug thudded against the window frame. There were no tentative scritch-scratchings or inquisitive faces pressed up against the cracked window this time, just two flumpy-thumps which surprised Dotta so much she let her apron fall to the floor.

"Flaggermusses?" she called out. "Wass mattoori?"

The little bats picked themselves up from the window-ledge and, panting from their rapid flight throughout the cold night, climbed up the side of the frame as quickly as their little thumbs and feet could take them, jabbering in bat-speak as they did so. Dotta reached up and let them into the warm room, where they whizzed to her shoulders and both squeaked shrilly in unison:

"**A whale!**"

"Walloo?" Dotta repeated, puzzled.

"**Yes! A whale!**"

"Nay!"

"**Yes!**"

"Walloo in vorter?"

"**Yes, yes, yes!**" The bats shrieked in frustration.

"Ver in vorter?"

"**In the fjord. In the inlet! In the harbour!**"

"Nay!"

By this time, the poor flaggermusses were beside themselves. They left Dotta's shoulders and began swooping and circling around the room, dipping low and then zooming up high, trying to show her how they had swept over the surface of the water to investigate.

Dotta's head was in a spin. She just did not understand. She had heard tales before of the odd whale getting lost and straying into an inlet, but never really believed them. It just didn't make sense. Why would a whale make a mistake like that? And this flaggermuss story was surely ridiculous. A whale would never stray out of ocean waters to swim near the anchored fishing boats in the harbour. Never so close to the Big People. The idea was crazy.

However, Dotta felt uneasy. The bats always knew what was going on and they were never wrong. What if there really was a whale in the inlet? How would it return to the open sea? How would it know which way to swim? Could it turn around?

The thought of a trapped whale made Dotta shake. How could anyone help? With trembling hands and a thumping heart, she struggled to open the old door to call Grimhildr from her work. The bats flew on ahead of her and by the time Dotta had hobbled over the snow, Grimhildr had worked it out.

"Es verisht badli foor walloo," she muttered darkly as they made for the little shack together. "Biggy Menor catchen en choppen walloo. Biggy Menor es hungeror."

Dotta's shaking hand flew to her face. This had not occurred to her. Ever since their conversation with Halvor, she had pushed the idea out of her mind. Until Grimhildr had spoken, her only concern was that the whale was trapped and would need turning and releasing. This was now an altogether different emergency.

"Nay, nay, Grimhildr! Biggy Menor nics eatig walloo!" she began to sob. "Pleasor, helpen walloo!"

"Hor, Hildi? Hor?" Grimhildr questioned, throwing her arms in the air, hopelessness washing over her, sapping her of her usual strength.

One turned to face the other in the bitter cold and they both grasped hands. Dotta desperately searched for an answer in Grimhildr's eyes, but found none. United in anguish and distress, the two she-trolls helped each other back into their home.

~~~

Sly-Erik, son of Slyvor the Whale-Boner and grandson of Slyvic the Whale-Jabber, raised his hand for silence. His sharp eyes narrowed as he drew a wheezing breath to speak. A hush fell over the thronging crowd of Big People gathered inside and outside the inn at the harbour's edge. All waited expectantly.

"My friends," he greeted them, with a sinister smile. "Today, we have been given an opportunity!"

The crowd immediately cheered and clapped. Once more, Sly-Erik raised his hand.

"We have been given the opportunity to take what Njord, the Viking god of the sea himself, has offered us!"

Again, the crowd cheered.

"Was he not the one who brought good luck to sailors on our seas in years gone by?"

"YES! YES!"

Sly-Erik looked down at the crowd from his platform by the bar and soaked up the adulation.

"Did my father and my grandfather, and their fathers before them, not put their faith in Njord as they battled with the ocean waters and the deepest of the deep?"

"YES! YES!" the crowd shouted once more.

"We have been saved from near starvation by the mercy of Njord!"

"N – JORD! N – JORD!" the crowd chanted.

Sly-Erik nodded in time to the rhythm of the voices and waited for their zeal to calm. He knew he had the towns-people on his side. He knew how desperate they were for food. He knew they would listen to him. He relished the thrill of power and basked in its glory. His whaling knowledge was matched by no-one. Only he had the skills passed from generation to generation, as his family had been supreme hunters for as long as anyone could recall. None of *his* predecessors had lost their lives fighting to capture these huge beasts of the icy depths, although many others had. His grandfather had become a legend for leading countless men on the open sea in whaling boats with harpoons at the ready; his father had been applauded for bringing wealth and success to the community. Sly-Erik himself had survived many exhausting and treacherous sailings, and the loss of his right leg had only gained him even more respect. Now, he stood before a mass of people who had turned to him for guidance.

It had been a long time since Sly-Erik had taken his boat out with a strong crew to hunt for whales. His frustration at being prevented from doing what he and his family held so dear knew no bounds. He had ranted and beat the table with his fists when he heard how laws had been changed. He had no interest in falling whale numbers, or the sentimental feelings of people who did not understand his way of life. He had no interest in other countries, other cultures, other ways of trading and eating. He had no interest in anything other than whaling. If he could no longer hunt whales, he felt he was finished and all his family's expertise would be lost for ever. Since he had stopped whaling, his standing in the community had become less significant. He used to be idolised by these people.

This trapped whale presented an opportunity.

An opportunity to regain respect.

An opportunity to be important once more.

Sly-Erik cleared his throat and the men, women and children before him were silenced. He dragged and clicked his wooden leg along the platform. The people waited.

"I will bring you this whale," he promised with grim determination. His voice was low and grating. "I know how hungry you are. I know you must eat. All I need is a sturdy crew of men." He paused and cast his sharp eyes over them.

There was a murmur amongst the crowd and people glanced nervously from one to the other. Some men shuffled their feet awkwardly as their wives nudged them. Children tugged at their fathers' sleeves and looked imploringly up at them. They were all thinking the same thing, but none dared speak out.

"Are you with me or not?" questioned Sly-Erik, his tone becoming harsher. "If you are man enough, step forward! Do you want to starve?" He fixed them with a piercing stare and tapped his wooden leg on the floor in impatience.

Tap. Tap. Tap.

A voice spoke out strongly from the back of the room.

"We cannot do this."

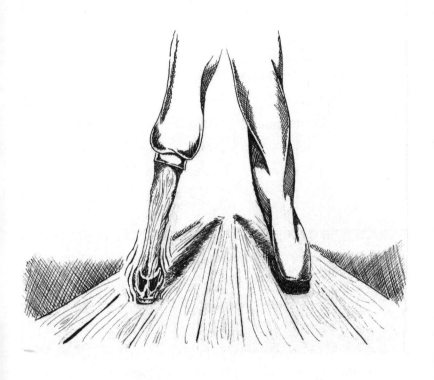

...tapped his wooden leg on the floor in impatience...

A gasp ran through the listening people. Who had challenged Sly-Erik?

"We have a ban."

It had been said. What everyone was privately thinking had been spoken. No-one was comfortable with going against the new laws.

Sly-Erik up drew his wiry frame and peered through the crowd. His left eye twitched. His mouth curled into a snarl.

"Who speaks against me?" he demanded.

As one, the people parted, looking back towards the door. There stood a bearded man with a chocolate-brown gundog at his side. He had a firm hand on her bluebell collar.

"I do," Halvor said quietly. "We *must* find another way. Whether we agree with the ban or not, we cannot break the law."

"The law is WRONG!" boomed Sly-Erik.

"Whale numbers have been falling," Halvor responded, trying to sound calm but feeling a tremor of fear inside. "We must let the stocks build up or there will be no food in the future."

"But this is a MINKE!" Sly-Erik bawled, incredulous that he should have anyone in disagreement with him. **"They are not endangered in our waters!"** Then he stooped to address the people directly in front of him. "Anyway," he added with an unpleasant snarl, "who's going to dare tell?"

The crowd became uncomfortable. They wanted to hunt, but knew they shouldn't. They were hungry, but frightened. They wanted a strong leader to guide them, but their initial eagerness was waning with these few words from Halvor. Sly-Erik felt the change in mood and wrestled to regain control.

"Remember, all of you, when you tuck your children up in bed at night, **you** are responsible for their tears. You could fill their bellies. Be warned, this whale has been delivered to us by Njord and we should not be ungrateful to him!"

Men and women held their children closer and Sly-Erik could see heads nodding.

"I need four good men behind me," he continued, now completely ignoring Halvor as the crowd closed around him once more. "These men may have to face more than the whale if the authorities find out. Decide amongst yourselves who is fearless enough. You know where to find me."

With that, the meeting ended. Sly-Erik made his way out, the people stepping back to allow him to drag and tap past.

Drag – tap. Drag – tap. Drag – tap.

He paused for a second to fix Halvor with a stare.

Eyes met eyes. Sly-Erik did not blink.

A shiver ran down Halvor's spine.

He felt powerless.

~~~

Confusion ~

The dancing lights which rippled on the surface of the water, and occasionally darted below, had stopped with the grey dawn. The alien, hostile noises and hurled stones which had rained down in the night had died away. Now, at last, he could risk breaching without panic sending him into a deep dive. Now, all that remained was an unnerving quiet.

The minke should have felt calmer.

He didn't.

It was true, the water felt slightly warmer than the crushed ice depths he had shared with his mother, but it no longer felt welcoming. There was an uneasy silence in this part of the sea. There were no distant whale calls. There were no shoals of herring or sardines darting past. There were no familiar sensations of any sort. The young minke began to realise that this was an area of the world that his mother had not prepared him for. They had not experienced this part of the sea together. This was completely new territory. And he was completely alone.

Grunts and whistles that he sent out brought no response.

It seemed that even the fish did not wish to venture near here. Perhaps they knew something he didn't.

The whale instinctively had an urge to return to the open ocean, and the safety of being lost in its greatness. Whilst before he had felt vulnerable there without his mother at his side, now he needed more space, more depth in which to dive, more freedom to swim and blow without strange, threatening sounds and shapes frightening him into twists and turns. With new determination, his tail flukes powering down the inlet, he swam, hoping to meet the sea.

Instead, he met ancient stone which formed harbour walls; he met sunken boats with rusted anchors.

He did not understand. He lost all sense of direction.

Chapter Six

*G*ruffle-snuffle. Snuffle-gruffle.

Dotta recognised Tracker's dog noises outside the door of the shack before Hildi's tappity-tap rang out. She wiped a last tear from her eye, blew her nose hurriedly and, patting her wispy hair in place, went to let them in.

"Gooshty morgy, Dotta! Halloo, Tracker!" she exclaimed in relief at seeing her sister-troll. Hildi and she hugged warmly, whilst Tracker bounded into the little room to greet the sleepy breakfast animals and help them lick their dishes clean. Thom followed, holding his strong hand out to clasp Dotta's. Grimhildr threw morning-chopped kindling onto the fire making it flare and crackle, before greeting the visitors. It was good to be together, sharing the warmth.

Hildi had brought some Troll-Cherry Wine with her. She had heard that it was needed for some concoction, and so she passed Dotta a dainty blue bottle from the bottom of her basket. Tailo and Scratchen fell out onto the floor in a flurry of black and brown fuzz. They scampered off in search of cheese and bread bits so easily found in cracks and corners.

"Verisht gooshty, Hildi," Dotta said, as she pulled out the bottle stopper with a satisfying pop and inhaled deeply. "Thanken, thanken, mi lovelor sistoori!"

"Es verisht speshy en strongish, Dotta," Hildi warned. For some reason, the cherries for this particular batch had been fuller in flavour and darker in colour. The result was powerful. "Nics drinkoosh mooch!"

"Nay, nay," Dotta replied with a smile. "Nay worrish. Es foor mi Shloopish. Es marvellurg!" and she popped it into her apron pocket. This could just be the Final Ingredient.

Once comfortable, sitting in the sturdy wooden chairs, nettle tea steaming gently, the trolls discussed the bats' sighting of the whale in the inlet. The sister-trolls were despondent. Thom listened to their concerns carefully. He shook his head and sighed.

"Es verisht badli foor walloo," he agreed. "Biggy Menor hab hungeror. Hungeror menor es dedden foor walloo." Thom looked serious. "Walloo es shtuk."

They all sipped their tea, cupping their hands around it for comfort, lost in thought. Some things, it seemed, were out of their control.

It was Tracker who broke the silence. He suddenly scrambled to his feet and gave a bark, ears cocked and eyes bright, nose straining towards the door. His tail began to wag expectantly. Grimhildr stood up and peered through the little window.

There, striding through the forest snow, was Halvor. He was wrapped up warmly with a chunkily knitted scarf and great padded gloves, which made his hands look even larger than usual. His huge boots kept sinking into the white depths and he had a stout walking stick with him. Limping along beside him was Kishi. She struggled to keep up the pace as the snow was so deep in places, and Halvor had to keep stopping to allow her to catch up. Although he was gentle with his dog, he seemed to be in a hurry and Grimhildr frowned as she watched them approach. There had to be a very important reason for Halvor to bring Kishi out in these conditions.

~~~

The dark boathouse smelled of damp wellies and stale fish. Oily ropes lay in twisted knots on the sodden floor. A grimy lantern swung from a hook on the ceiling, giving a dull orange glow in contrast to the bright snow falling outside.

Sly-Erik sat in a corner, as quiet as a waiting spider, except for the **tap – tap – tap** of his wooden leg. He was in no particular rush. He could wait. He knew the men would come. He just had to bide his time and plan.

Tap. Tap. Tap.

~~~

"I *thought* you would know about the whale," Halvor commented, looking grim.

"The flaggermusses told us," replied Grimhildr, taking lead in the conversation as she knew that Dotta tired easily of speaking Big People's language, and that she was already upset. "We have been trying to think of a way to turn him around and encourage him out to sea, but it is so difficult. Maybe nature and whale instincts will lead him."

Dotta shuffled away from the group and tended to her wolverine, taking the opportunity to pet Kishi who was happily sniffing noses with Tracker. If she couldn't help the whale, she must busy herself with things that would help the other animals. She reached into her apron pocket and started to gather ingredients from her cupboard. Soon she was lost in a fragrant cloud of bubbling brew.

"I'm afraid we haven't got time to wait for either nature or whale instincts," Halvor continued.

"There has been a development and that's why I am here."

Grimhildr *knew* there had been a good reason for this visit. She cast a concerned glance at Hildi and Thom. Hildi had her hands clasped tightly, resting on the table top. Her bright eyes were anxious and she looked to her troll-man for guidance. Thom was frowning. It was as if he had guessed.

"I have said to you all that I will always be in your debt for looking after dear Kishi when she was trapped in the forest," Halvor began. "I have promised to help you if ever I could."

The trolls nodded but stayed quiet.

"I know you are always wanting to protect the living and that you cherish all creatures, from the tiniest beetle under a rock, to the huge whales that navigate distant waters. As you know, Big People are not always like that."

He paused and looked with fondness and anxiety at the trolls around him. How was he to explain the whale's predicament to these earnest, caring faces?

"The whale is in mortal danger," he almost whispered.

Thom nodded. It was as he had thought.

"Big Men?" he queried.

Halvor nodded, his great bushy beard almost sweeping the table top.

"The people are desperate for food. They have been told that this whale is a gift to them, and that they should not upset Njord by refusing it. They have been asked to gather a group of strong men so that they can go out in a whaling boat and... and... and..." Halvor swallowed.

"KILL IT?" shouted Grimhildr, unable to contain herself. Thom clenched his fists. Dotta dropped her Shloopish spoon with a clatter. Spats of her special sleeping potion scattered stickily on to the floor. Tailo and Scratchen, never ones to miss an opportunity, scurried over to lick at them, greedily. They were completely unaware of the tension in the little room.

"You have to understand," Halvor tried to explain. "Whale meat is normal for these people. It is just the same as you fishing in the fjord. They really don't want to do anything wrong, but..." Halvor's voice trailed off.

"But?" Hildi asked.

"Not only are the people starving, *but* also they are being led by Sly-Erik."

"Sly-Erik?" the trolls repeated as one.

"I'm afraid so, and he is hungry in quite a different way." Halvor took a great slurp of his tea before continuing. The trolls almost held their breath. Halvor stared into their eyes.

"He is hungry for… **power!**"

"I don't understand," murmured Hildi. "What does that mean? Power over what? Why?"

"Power over the people. He wants to be in charge. He wants to be important like his forefathers have been. He sees this as an opportunity to win respect from the towns-people. If he can bring them food, especially by saying that Njord would wish it, he hopes they will look up to him and make him feel special."

Halvor really hoped the trolls would understand. This whole idea was so alien to them and their way of life, they might not believe him. He needn't have worried.

"So, he wants control," Thom muttered darkly. "Nothing surprises me when it comes to Big People."

Halvor flushed under his beard. Hildi was quick to notice his discomfort.

"Halvor, don't worry. We know *you* are not like this!"

"Nor am I easily led!" the Big Man retorted. "I have already spoken against Sly-Erik and said we must not do this! Men must not join in with his plan! I told him we should find another way to get food!"

"And? And?" the trolls cried.

Halvor looked down, suddenly crestfallen. "I think I have made myself an enemy," he said quietly.

~~~

Tap. Tap. Tap.

Sly-Erik waited.

Tap. Tap. Tap.

Sly-Erik plotted.

Tap. Tap. Tap.

Sly-Erik smiled.

~~~

Dotta found her pipes. A soothing tune was needed. It was the only thing she could think of doing. Halvor was troubled. Grimhildr and Thom were angry. Hildi was alarmed. The lilting troll-melody would calm everyone, including herself. It would help them to clear their minds and think. The notes floated down upon them like gentle petals. The animals relaxed and laid their heads on their paws, or tucked them under their wings. The trolls nodded their heads, just so, and rocked in time.

The mice slept.

Flat out.

In the middle of the floor, on their backs.

Snoring.

Thom listened to the music and looked at the mice. Puzzled, he turned to the other animals who, although resting, were not actually asleep. He looked back at Tailo and Scratchen. They were sleeping like babies. Tailo's fat, brown tummy rose and fell as he dreamed of cloudberries and crunchy nuts. Scratchen twitched and snitched his way through dream tunnels and fields of corn. Suddenly, Thom raised his hairy hand to signal to Dotta to stop playing. She brought her tune to an abrupt halt and Thom jumped to his feet.

"Dee Shloopish!" he cried. "Dee littelor morsies dreamoori! Looki!"

They all turned to look at the mice. There was no doubt about it; they were absolutely out of it. Tracker got up from his place by Kishi's side and nudged Tailo gently with his nose. A whistling noise issued from the mouse's tiny pursed lips, followed by a contented sigh and a chomping of his teeth as he turned over and curled up into a tight ball.

Dotta whooped and clapped her hands in delight! When neither mouse stirred, she just knew she had a special sleeping potion that worked.

"Marvellurg!" she exclaimed. "Dee morsies nics varken oop!"

Grimhildr was pleased. It had taken so long for Dotta to achieve this and now, at last, she had success. The mice seemed to be very peaceful and happy, completely oblivious to the world. She realised they must have licked just a few drops of the special sleeping potion, which had been just enough for little mice to fall asleep. Now, all they had to do was to work out how much bigger the other animals were, to have the right dose to help *them* to sleep. This meant that she and Dotta could tend to animals' needs without distress. Wonderful!

Thom looked across at Halvor, Dotta's sweet piping notes still ringing in his ears.

"I think I might have a plan," he whispered quietly.

~~~

Steinarr was the first to arrive at the boathouse, throwing open the door with a deafening **whack!** Sly-Erik had recognised the pounding of his feet as he thundered along the quayside towards him. Steinarr stood full-square in the doorway and blocked out the light. He blinked in the relative gloom of the room, trying to make out the dark shapes.

Tap. Tap. Tap.

"AH, SLY-ERIK, *THERE* YOU ARE!" he boomed.

Tap. Tap. Tap.

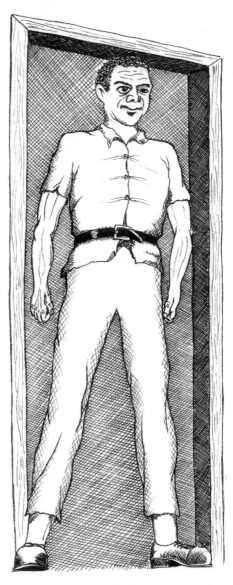

...Steinarr stood full-square in the doorway...

"I'VE COME TO CAPTURE THE STINKY MINKE, I HAVE! I WANT TO BASH HIM AND EAT HIM, I DO!"

"So it would seem," came Sly-Erik's voice from the corner. "Welcome, Steinarr, Man of Stone! Come join me at the table and we'll talk."

The hulking man lumbered over and heaved himself down onto an old barrel that groaned beneath his weight. Sly-Erik tapped his way to a battered, throne-like chair at the head of the table.

"I THINK MORE MEN ARE COMING, THEY ARE!" yelled Steinarr.

Sly-Erik grimaced and put his hands to his ears, then looking right and left, put a finger to his lips.

"Shhhhhh! You make my ears ring! And we don't want anyone to tell the authorities what we are doing!"

Steinarr looked confused and his left eye began to squint. With great effort, he lowered his voice into a grumbling sort of growl. "People already know our plan, they do, and they agree with it." He nodded his great head slowly. "Oh, yes! No doubt about it. They are expecting you to deliver the whale to them, they are!"

"And so I will," promised Sly-Erik, patiently. "So I will. But we have to plan our action, you know.

We can't just blunder out there in a boat and make a wild stab at the sea!"

Steinarr drew himself up on his barrel. "I can!" he announced proudly. "I'm really good at wild stabbing, I am!" and he made fierce jabbing movements with fist clenched. "Like this, see? Jab! Stab! Spear! Spear! Doof! Doof!"

"No, no, no!" insisted Sly-Erik, beginning to wish he had personally selected his men rather than just asking for volunteers. "You must follow *instructions* and be part of a *crew*. Wait for others to come and I will tell you what to do."

Fortunately for Sly-Erik, no sooner had he said these words than there was a loud knocking at the door of the boathouse.

"Come!" called Sly-Erik loudly.

The malevolent form of Belgr entered. He walked with a heron-like stoop, a long, black cloak protecting him from the winter chill. He extended a thin, bony hand from beneath the wrappings and Sly-Erik clasped it.

"Well, well, Belgr," he said with a knowing smile. "I thought you would join me. We go back a long way, do we not?"

...The malevolent form of Belgr entered...

"Indeed, we do," replied the hunched, old friend.

"We have many years of experience behind us, don't we?" continued Sly-Erik.

"Indeed, we do," came the response, and Belgr seated himself at Sly-Erik's right hand.

"You know Steinarr?"

"Indeed, I do," Belgr answered. He cast an eye at Steinarr and acknowledged him with a brief nod.

"So now we have brains and brawn, who else will arrive, I wonder?" Sly-Erik mused. They all waited in silence, slow minutes tapping by.

Tap. Tap. Tap.

~~~

In the little forest shack, Halvor and Thom stayed at the table, earnestly talking. Dotta and Grimhildr busied themselves with the animals, giving instructions to Hildi who was a willing helper. Tracker and Kishi frolicked in the snow outside, kicking billowing clouds of white powder into the air and snapping at freshly-falling flakes. They were carefree and happy.

Unlike the trolls and Halvor, who were deeply troubled.

They all knew time was of the essence.

They all knew that Thom was good at planning.

They just didn't know whether his plans would work, or if they could be carried out before Sly-Erik made his move.

~~~

Desperation and acceptance ~

The young minke was growing tired. He had thrashed up and down the inlet but was disorientated and confused. He no longer knew which way led to the open sea.

He had sent out whistles and grunts; he had desperately hoped for replies; he recognised that he was missing the guiding shadow of his mother whale. He had tried again and again to regain some sense of his surroundings, to no avail.

And now he was tired.

He swam disconsolately, without his original joy and fervour on experiencing the ocean depths for the first time, and now without his passion to find an escape. His desperation had exhausted him. He had found no fish to eat and was feeling weak with hunger.

He plunged to a new depth; acceptance of defeat.

Chapter Seven

S quelch, squish! Squish, squelch!

Galmann's dirty, waterlogged boots announced his arrival. His wild, ragged hair was as mad as usual and his popping eyes bulged scarily as he greeted the others, mutely. Although born without the ability to speak, he made himself easily understood in other ways. The other Big Men noted, with some relief, that his well-used hunting knife was safely sheathed for the time-being. Valdrik accompanied him; the two were always together. Galmann could *never* be left on his own.

He could *never, ever* be trusted.

Valdrik acted as his guard. Valdrik could control Galmann's vicious tendencies – *most* of the time. He was the only man deemed tough enough. Together, they made an alarming pair.

They were perfect for Sly-Erik.

Now the team was complete and orders could be given.

The five Big Men huddled round the fish-gutting table, unaffected by the rancid smell which seeped from the wood. Sly-Erik set out his plan for the following night. There was plenty to do; the boat would have to be made ready; the threatened storm would have to be considered; the time of tides would have to be worked out. There were weapons to bring out of store and check. They would have to ensure every rope was oiled and secure. Protective clothing would have to be gathered from below decks and sturdy non-slip boots found. Squelchy wellies would not be strong enough – nor would they grip the sea-washed deck as they battled against whale and weather.

"We don't have long," warned Sly-Erik grimly. "We must prepare quickly, before the whale finds his way back to the open ocean."

The men nodded in agreement, Steinarr's left eye squinting with the effort of concentration. The list of jobs seemed long and hard to complete.

"I WILL TRY MY BEST, I WILL!" he bellowed to the group. "I WANT TO JAB HIM AND STAB HIM, I DO!"

"Shhh!" Sly-Erik hissed. "Keep your booming voice down, Man of Stone! I appreciate your fervour, Steinarr, but we have to take care!"

"Indeed, we do," Belgr muttered, scowling darkly. He hunched his withered shoulders further back into his cloak and grimaced. He had serious doubts about this team. It was not like in the old days…

Valdrik cleared his throat and fixed Sly-Erik with a meaningful stare.

"It is not only the boat, the weather, the ropes and so on that we have to worry about though, is it?" he asked, fully knowing the answer.

Sly-Erik tapped his leg in irritation at being reminded. The two Big Men fixed each other with cold, granite eyes.

Tap. Tap. Tap.

"Halvor…" they said in bitter unison.

~~~

The trolls, too, were making plans and preparations, knowing that time was against them. They discussed Thom's ideas feverishly into the night. There was so much to do! They suspected correctly, that the Big Men would be gathering and organising the kill over the following day, so the trolls, too, had just one day to get ready. As the gloom of the winter sky became darker, they allocated different tasks to each one of them so they could prepare as efficiently as possible. Teamwork was essential. All had a vital role to play if they were to stand any chance of saving the lost minke. By the end of their evening together, the trolls and Halvor felt far from confident but absolutely determined.

"Good night to you all," Halvor said, gathering scarf, gloves and a reluctant Kishi. She gazed at

Tracker with eyes of melting chocolate and took her place at her master's side. "I will return tomorrow when the little bats tell me that all is ready. Good luck, my dear friends. You have a hard mission ahead of you."

The old door closed with a dull thud and they were gone.

Without the presence of the gentle Big Man, the trolls suddenly felt very much on their own. It seemed easy to be bold when he was with them. Thom turned away from the closed door and looked at the three sisters.

"Hildi, Dotta en Grimhildr," he addressed them, "nay worrish! Ve hab littlelor leggors ub ve es strongish. Ve helpen walloo. Ve *willen* helpen walloo!"

"Yo, yo!" they replied in earnest. "In morgy, ve starterig!"

With that, Hildi and Thom took their leave, Tracker bounding through the snow at their heels, mice safely in Hildi's basket, still snoring sweetly. The forest night enveloped them as they disappeared into the trees.

~~~

Mistig Vorter lay perfectly still as Thom approached early next morning. It could not bob its usual greeting. The little boat had not been taken out on the water for weeks and was iced up with the intense cold. The oars were solidly frozen in a shining mirror which covered the bottom, and some snow was heaped at the prow. Grateful for the winter fur which had grown over his hands, Thom scooped the drift out hurriedly and tried to tug one oar free. His fingers grappled against the ice, struggling for grip. He managed to work a small hole around it and, leaning back, tugged with all his might. With a splintering crack, the ice gave way and at last Thom staggered backwards, oar in hand. The second oar followed more easily and the ice could be pulled away like shards of glass. Thom would never have thought of taking Mistig Vorter out onto the fjord in these conditions normally, but this was an emergency. He could think of no other solution. His noble, little boat would have to be ready to serve him well that night. There would be only one chance.

Whilst Thom struggled, Hildi gathered her remaining bottles of Troll-Cherry Wine and six fillets of summer-smoked fish which hung amongst the dried herbs in her kitchen. A loaf of rye bread went alongside them in her basket. Putting a dish of crumbs and some cheese gratings next to the dozy mice, ready for when they awoke, she clicked her tongue at Tracker and set off down the path. Grimo, the smoky-grey cat, shuddered as the door closed behind them. He had been out for just a few minutes each day for weeks now – and only when absolutely desperate – the snow too numbing for his dainty pink pads. Quite why That Dog loved romping through it so much, he couldn't understand. But then there were lots of things he didn't understand about dogs.

Many fine cheeses were stacked in the cold store. Grimhildr knew they were all delicious, so it didn't matter which one she selected. The nearest fell from the wooden shelf into her hands. It was ripe and gave the promise of an oozing centre once opened. Perfect. Irresistible. She tucked it under her hairy armpit and made her way to her tool shed. She needed to gather all that she would be able to carry. Her face was set in a hard frown of determination. Their plan just *had* to work.

~~~

Sly-Erik summoned Galmann and Valdrik to him. The others grumbled as they left. If they were to make ready the whaling boat, they needed all hands and hoped the madman and his guard would not be long. Belgr watched Steinarr in irritation as he blundered his way around the deck. This man might be strong, but had no wits about him. As far as Belgr was concerned, he was a bad choice.

"I'M REMEMBERING ALL THE JOBS ON MR ERIK'S LIST, I AM!" Steinarr shouted, as the wind howled around them. "I CAN'T WAIT TO GET TO THAT WHALE, I CAN'T! I'M EXCITED, I AM!"

"Indeed," replied Belgr, inspecting the end of a harpoon with an experienced eye.

"I DON'T KNOW WHY THE OTHERS AREN'T HELPING, I DON'T! I THINK THEY SHOULD DO THEIR SHARE, I DO!"

Belgr made no comment. He knew exactly why Galmann and Valdrik had been sent for. He and Sly-Erik had continued discussions long after the others had left the night before. They always worked well together, and the final part of their plan had to be sorted out. It was difficult but not impossible, this *Halvor* complication. Both knew that he was the one member of the town who was opposed to the slaughter. Both knew that he would do what he could in order to protect the whale.

He had to be silenced.

He had to be stopped.

~~~

Dotta was in a flap.

Her job that day was of such vital importance that she felt the responsibility to get it right was almost too much for her. She had the shack to herself as Grimhildr was busy outside, but despite this, it seemed impossible to think straight and keep her mind clear.

"Oh dearig, dearig," she muttered in concern. "Dee Shloopish es trickoori!"

It was essential that she remembered the recipe. She had to get the right combination of ingredients, and then double or even treble the amounts if it was going to work. She would have to watch the fire to make sure it was the right heat. She would have to make sure she kept alert and didn't set apron strings alight. She would have to stand over the bubbling brew the whole time to ensure it didn't boil over, and that would make her little, short legs and hairy knees ache *so* much. She felt her track record in special sleeping potion-making was not too good so far, and would have liked another practice run before making the real thing. She fretted and worried her way around the tiny kitchen as she gathered what she thought she needed. Had she used dandelion last time? Did she have any liquorice root left? Was it clover honey or heather honey?

It was only when Hildi arrived with her basket of food that Dotta began to calm down.

"Dotta, Dotta, shhh! U mekken marvellurg Shloopish. Nay worrish!" Hildi soothed her sister. "Looki – Im helpen u."

So saying, Hildi rolled up her sleeves and passed bottles and pots from the cupboard. Her cheerful manner was not a true reflection of how she felt, though. It was imperative that Dotta *did* get it right this time. No room for error at all.

Halvor's life might depend on it.

~~~

The sudden thundering blows at Halvor's door made Kishi scramble under the bed, shaking with fear.

Without waiting for an answer, Galmann forced entry and stood looking crazed and excitable on the threshold. His left hand was outstretched towards Halvor, fingers opening and closing into a fist, as if to grasp him. His right hand clenched the fearsome hunting knife which was his constant companion. He stared madly around him, grinning with rotten teeth. A few drops of spit began to spill over on to his bottom lip.

Valdrik pushed past him to confront a terrified Halvor.

"W–w–what do you want?" Halvor managed to stutter, his heart beating so hard that he could hear it thumping in his chest. He swallowed to keep a wave of sickness at bay, wiping the sweat from his hands onto his trousers.

Valdrik smiled. He turned to Galmann.

"Did you hear that, Galmann?" The madman grinned and thrust his knife forwards. Valdrik continued, his tone threateningly controlled, "Halvor is so keen to please us that he asks us what we want, the very moment we arrive!" Galmann grinned even more widely and began to nod his head up and down, his grey tongue hanging out like a dog panting. A long drool of spit snaked its way to the floor.

"I–I–I am n–n–not pleased to see you!" Halvor stammered. "Tell me what you w–w–want and g–go!"

Valdrik took a further stride into the room. Galmann followed, grasping hand still outstretched, gurgling now with anticipation. Halvor stepped backwards and positioned himself behind the sturdy table. He tried to calculate how he could reach the door to escape, but Galmann was blocking it.

Valdrik stared, unblinking into Halvor's eyes. His face appeared expressionless.

"It's not a case of what *I* want," he answered, pausing to enjoy the look of fear on Halvor's face. Beads of sweat had appeared on his victim's forehead, and he could see the rising panic in his eyes.

...his grey tongue hanging out like a dog panting...

"W–what, then?" Halvor pleaded.

Valdrik almost whispered his reply. "It's a case of what *Sly-Erik* wants…"

Halvor swallowed again. He felt as if he had been kicked in the guts. His legs became suddenly weak and he felt as if he might drop to the floor at any moment. He was incapable of speech.

"What do you think, Galmann?" Valdrik addressed his wild friend. "Should we tell him what Sly-Erik wants?"

Galmann sucked his spittle back through his brown teeth and wiped his loose lips on his sleeve. Again, he nodded furiously. Halvor looked from one to the other, panic now consuming him like a hot fire.

Valdrik savoured the moment.

"Sly-Erik wants you to come with us."

Halvor shook his head. This he must not do. All their plans would be for nothing if he went to Sly-Erik's just now. Later, yes, but not yet. For a second, Valdrik showed a flash of irritation. He was not used to being disobeyed.

"Are you refusing?" he questioned. "Do you DARE to refuse a request from the Sly-One?"

Halvor gulped. He had to think fast. Kishi whined from her hiding place. Galmann immediately dropped to his knees to search for her. Halvor saw this and his brain switched into gear.

"I can't come – yet," he managed to answer.

Valdrik raised an eyebrow.

"I can't come y–yet because I am expected down in the town," Halvor lied in a sudden rush. "The people will miss me and come to look for me."

Valdrik hesitated. He did not want anyone arriving at Sly-Erik's door until the night's deed was done. A delay could mean they miss the tide, and the whale.

"Sly-Erik wants you before the day is over," Valdrik replied. "He will not be happy with you if you do not arrive!"

Halvor glanced at Galmann. The madman had located Kishi and was crawling on his hands and knees towards the bed, knife clamped in his teeth.

"T–tell Sly-Erik I will come!" Halvor almost shouted, unable to stop staring in horror at Galmann. "Tell him I will be there early this evening!"

Valdrik followed the direction of Halvor's eyes and understood.

"Very well," he smiled. He looked over to Galmann once more. "Galmann? Have you found a wittle doggie-woggie?"

The Big Man on the floor turned his head in reply and slathered through gritted teeth.

"I expect you'd like a wittle doggie-woggie to play with, wouldn't you, Galmann?" Valdrik continued as Halvor listened in terror. Once more, Galmann nodded and began to shuffle forward. Valdrik fixed Halvor with a steely stare.

"Don't disappoint me, Halvor," he said in a threatening tone of voice. "I know where your dog lives."

Halvor shook his head. "I won't. I promise!"

Just as Galmann reached out his hand to drag Kishi out by the tail, Valdrik called him to order. Dog-like himself, he obeyed, whimpering in disappointment.

Then they were gone.

~~~

Waiting ~

All this time, the Big People of the town were watching the young whale. They murmured amongst themselves, grimacing with the gnawing pain of hunger.

Out in the fjord, occasionally two blows were to be seen and heard as the minke breathed, but they sounded like ponderous sighs from the depths of his soul.

A white diamond-patch broke the surface of the water and slowly,

so very slowly,

circled, before…

sinking

out

of

sight.

Chapter Eight

*D*rip, drop. Dribble, drobble.

The last drips of Dotta's special sleeping potion were scraped from the steaming cooking pot. Three ruby bottles were corked and placed side-by-side on the table in the kitchen, and the troll-sisters stood back to admire the crimson glow of their work. All the Troll-Cherry Wine was used up.

"Verisht gooshty Shloopish, Dotta," Hildi commented.

"Yo, yo, Hildi," Dotta replied with satisfaction, nodding her head. "Thanken foor ur helpen. Im verisht pleasorig."

The scent of the special sleeping potion had filled the air in the tiny room, and Dotta was feeling decidedly dozy and more relaxed. Her eyelids were drooping and she had a dreamy smile of relief on her gentle face.

"Im sitli en restig," she said, making her way to the comfortable fireside chair. Perhaps just a little snooze might be nice, just to rest her weary legs and knees. Just a little…

"Nay, nay, Dotta!" Hildi replied hurriedly. "Dee flaggermusses en dee peepors!" She grasped her sister's elbow just before she sank down onto the cushion. "Halvor en dee walloo!"

This urgent reminder brought Dotta to her senses. Of course! She still had things to do. She must find her pipes and warm them with her sweet breath so that they would play beautifully when the time came. She must think hard to remember and practise the right sounds and notes. Before too long, she must gather her warm goat blanket and wrap it tightly around her, ready for her trip. She must not be late for Thom. Timing was going to be crucial.

Hildi threw open the window of the little shack to let the bracing late-afternoon air refresh them and Dotta plucked the sleepy bats from their roost. Pipi rubbed her little snout and peered blearily around the room. Fug sniffed at the fresh breeze and stretched his shiny wings. It seemed far too early for them to wake up. The light made their blackcurrant eyes water and blink.

"Findor Halvor, mi flaggermusses," Dotta urged them. "Fastli, fastli!"

Although the tiny bats understood *what* to do and took their leave through the open window, flitting quickly into the forest, they didn't understand *why*

133

they had to do it. They did not know that their arrival at Halvor's home was the signal he was waiting for. They did not know that he was pacing the floor, hoping they would arrive before he had to go to Sly-Erik. They did not know that their arrival was to set off a chain of carefully planned events which might – or might not – make all the difference to a young minke whale trapped in desperate, dark waters.

~~~

Tap. Tap. Tap.
"I did tell him, Sly Erik…"

Tap. Tap. Tap.
"I'm sure he'll come…"

Tap. Tap. Tap.
"We threatened him like you said we must…"

Tap. Tap. Tap.
"Galmann will get the dog if he doesn't…"

Tap. Tap. Tap.
"He said early this evening…"

Tap. Tap. Tap.
"He will be here, I'm sure…"

Tap. Tap. Tap.
"I did tell him… Honest."

Tap. Tap. Tap.

~~~

Halvor was ready and waiting for the bats. He had spent the last hour peering through his cracked window down the road towards the forest. He had been watching for this signal. As soon as he saw the familiar darting and swooping, he pulled on his great gloves and hat, swung open his door and strode out into the snow. He carried a rough sack over one shoulder which held a sealed flagon of ale. Kishi padded at his side, anxiously looking to him for encouragement, concerned about his grim, determined expression. Halvor did not click his tongue at her or give the usual whistle. Kishi knew instinctively she should follow closely, obedient and loyal. Halvor made haste towards the trolls' home, knowing that he would be joining Sly-Erik and his men before long. He had to collect everything the trolls had prepared for him and then return as quickly as he could back to the town. And the boathouse.

"Halloo, Halvor!" Dotta greeted the Big Man as he arrived. "Everythingor es reddig foor u. Comli fastli!"

So saying, she guided him to the table where the special sleeping potion bottles stood. Next to them lay the great cheese that Grimhildr had brought inside, together with Hildi's smoked fish and rye bread. All ready and waiting.

"Oh!" Halvor exclaimed. "This looks wonderful! I am so hungry!" He allowed himself a long gaze at the bread and cheese. "They couldn't possibly resist!" he grinned and started to pack the food into his sack. The flagon was uncorked and the three bottles of special sleeping potion poured in carefully. Halvor swirled the mixture and sealed the flagon once more. Into the sack it went and he was ready to leave. He bade farewell to Kishi, who was going to stay in safety with the other animals and Hildi in the shack.

The sister-trolls were suddenly solemn. They gripped their right hands together then held them across their hearts.

"Gooshty luckor," they all murmured, heads bowed.

~~~

The late afternoon light was grey and the sky hung heavy and threatening. The fjord was silent. The deepest water looked inky black. Somewhere in the mountains, a wolf howled and the mournful sound made the hair on the back of Thom's neck prickle. He tucked his troll-tail into the back of his dungarees and pulled the collar of his little jacket up around his neck. Shivering and with chattering teeth, he untied Mistig Vorter's rope and climbed aboard. The small boat creaked as Thom pushed one oar against the bank to free it from the frozen mooring. It seemed unwilling to leave the shore and its wooden frame was stiff and stubborn.

"Mi dearig, lovelor boot," Thom coaxed, patting the seat beside him. "U helpen oos todagen, pleasor. Thanken, thanken mi marvellurg Mistig Vorter!"

Less reluctantly, the rowing boat carried Thom out onto open water and the troll turned the prow in the direction of the far bank. There was a small jetty there which lay beneath the trees. A path led from the jetty, twisting its way up and into the forest. Troll-feet had trodden that path many, many times and it was the most direct route to Grimhildr and Dotta's home. Thom strained to look ahead through the misty gloom which rose around him, hoping to catch a glimpse of Hildi's sisters. He felt nervous. Had all gone to plan so far? Had Halvor collected all he needed? Had Grimhildr gathered her tools? Had Dotta remembered her pipes? His oars dip-plipped in and out of the water as he went over the plan in his mind.

Grimhildr was the first to wave. Her old eyes were sharper than Dotta's, and she had been searching the fjord edge keenly for a sign of Thom and his boat. At last there they were!

"Halloo!" she shouted and, turning quietly to Dotta, she said: "Thom comli, sistoori. Hab u ur peepors?"

...His oars dip-plipped in and out of the water...

Dotta drew the little wooden pipes out from under the goat hair blanket which was wrapped snugly over her shoulders.

"Yo, yo, Grimhildr. Looki! Mi peepors shtay warmoosh."

Her sister nodded in satisfaction. For all that Dotta was a bit dozy at times, Grimhildr knew that she would always look after her precious pipes. It was important they stay warm to play properly. It would be disastrous if the wrong notes sounded.

Within a few minutes, the little blue boat had drawn up at the end of the jetty and Thom was extending a hairy hand to help the she-trolls on board. Grimhildr passed down a heavy poshtig of tools before clambering into Mistig Vorter to sit beside Dotta. She held her hickory stick upright and firm.

"Everythingor gooshty?" questioned Thom as they settled themselves.

"Nay worrish!" replied Dotta. "Everythingor gooshty."

As Thom started to row towards the Big People's harbour, he tried to conceal his concern for the sake of the other two. This idea was good in theory, but whether it would really work remained to be seen. To challenge Sly-Erik and his men was both brave and foolhardy. All the trolls had a different, but equally important, role. They would not all be working together and timing was critical. It was essential everything went to plan. If it went wrong, the consequences for them all would be dreadful.

~~~

"I SHALL GO AND LOOK FOR HIM IF YOU WANT, I SHALL!" offered Steinarr, making for the door of the boathouse. "WE MUST SET SAIL BEFORE TOO LONG, WE MUST!"

"Shhhh, Man of Stone!" hissed Sly-Erik. "Come back here and sit down. There is time still. I am counting the taps until the time is right."

"Indeed you are," nodded Belgr, with a note of irritation. The boathouse had been largely silent but for the **tap – tap – tap** of Sly-Erik's wooden leg for the last hour. Belgr and the other men had gathered to wait. It was testing their patience. At least the whaling boat had been made ready at last, Belgr mused. Weapons had been taken out of store and sharpened so they glinted viciously. Ropes were oiled and coiled securely on deck. They would quickly slip into place and wrap their prey as tightly as a spider entombing its fly. The waterproof clothing had been found, tested and checked for size. Although not all items fit as well as they might, they did offer some protection against the elements on a stormy, dark night with a particularly large, thrashing fish to catch. Belgr turned his thoughts to days and nights long gone, when he and Sly-Erik had fought so valiantly side-by-side to bring their quarry down. He sighed. Happy days!

Valdrik was becoming impatient. How long these last few hours seemed! He needed entertainment. He stared at his shipmates around the fish-gutting table and his gaze fell on Galmann.

"Are you hungry, Galmann?" Valdrik questioned.

At the sound of his name, the mad-man looked up suddenly from the tabletop he had been studying intently for quarter of an hour. His wild eyes brightened and he nodded vigorously. Spit fell in drops from his mouth, collecting in a frothy pool in front of him.

"How do you want your whale supper?" Valdrik continued. "In a casserole? Grilled steaks? Whale burger?"

Galmann's head was bouncing up and down as he grunted in excitement. Steinarr's stomach rumbled, the noise rolling around the empty boatshed like slow thunder.

"Kebabs, anyone?" asked Valdrik in an innocent tone. "Sausages?"

Belgr shuffled uncomfortably and rubbed his middle. Galmann took out his hunting knife and began to rise from the table to make for the door. His wide mouth had a foolish grin and his eyes were bulging. Steinarr's left eye began to squint in sudden concern.

"Tomato ketchup or brown sauce?"

At that, there was uproar. Galmann raced for the door ready to leap into the water outside and grapple the whale with his hunting knife and bare hands. Steinarr threw back his chair in an elephantine panic that there was a mad-man on the loose. Belgr scuttled away from the table and withdrew, hunched, into a corner, hidden by the hood of his cloak.

"ENOUGH!"

The scene froze.

For a few seconds, everything was still. And silent.

Then Belgr peeped out from his hood. Steinarr cautiously picked up his fallen chair. Galmann slathered his drool back into his mouth and made his way back to the table, next to Valdrik who looked at the thunderous Sly-Erik.

"I was only *asking*…" he said.

~~~

Whilst Hildi gave the goats their hay and chopped apples from a summer store, found grains for the partridge whose wing splint had now been removed, fed the dogs and encouraged the wolverine to eat bread soaked in milk rather than suck milk from a bottle, Mistig Vorter arrived at the Big Men's harbour. There was no-one around. All the towns-people were holed up in their homes, trying to keep warm, waiting for news of the whale capture.

With her usual strength, Grimhildr climbed out of the boat and Thom passed her the heavy poshtig of troll-tools. She paused to cast an eye over the boats that were anchored safe from wind and rain. Then she nodded to Thom and Dotta as they held hands over their hearts in a silent farewell. Dotta mouthed "Gooshty luckor" to her sister and they rowed away from her, hearts now beginning to pound. Each began to think the plan through. Hildi was keeping their home and animals safe; Grimhildr was in position and had her tools at the ready; Dotta and Thom were on the fjord. Now all they needed was for Halvor to arrive at the boathouse and play his part.

And they had to find the whale.

Dotta searched the surface of the water in vain. Her lip began to quiver.

~~~

Halvor took a deep breath as he stood outside the boathouse. The people inside were not his friends. They were his enemies. The last time he had seen Sly-Erik, Halvor had been fixed with a stare so full of hatred that it had sent a shiver down his spine and filled him with fear. Only today, he had Valdrik and the mad Galmann in his home. He had been terrified. Kishi had been in peril.

Now he had to face these enemies in one group.

By himself.

He had to find the courage to do so.

Halvor felt the outside of his sack and made out the shape of the contents. He had everything he needed. Now all he had to do was to walk in and make the plan work. He couldn't fail. It wasn't just the whale that would be in danger if he did. He had to think of his new friends, the gentle trolls of the forest and fjord.

He had to think of Kishi.

~~~

Dreaming ~

Vague memories swirled and danced.

Confused flurries of flippers and first salty-air breathing. A rush of foaming waves; crashing, bright flashes in the sunlight. The exhilaration of speed and free spirit. Sweet milk. Warm waters. Pounding into depths, so blue, so cool. Pushing up – and up – and up – to burst the surface, two blows and dive. Downwards, downwards, down.

Zip-slippery fish, so soft. So fast. Shimmering with rainbows of flavour. Delight and comfort. Move on – follow.

Then cold. So cold. Pearly ice. Glass cage. Alone.

Turn back slowly. Lonely. Lost. Forlorn hope.

Noise. Panic. Lights flashing. Water chopping.

Which way to turn? Which way to turn? Which way?

Deep, dark despair. Deepest of darkness.

But then… a mother's voice? A mother's call? How so?

Chapter Nine

*W*eeping. Peep-peeping. Toowip! Tooweep!

The notes from Dotta's pipes floated across the water. Thom rested his oars in the rowlocks so Mistig Vorter became quite still and calm.

Nothing.

No sign.

Thom picked up his oars once more and dip-plipped his way across the fjord. Dip-plip. Dip-plip. Dip-plip.

With trembling lips, Dotta picked up her pipes and continued to play her whale song. She willed the minke to hear her with every faltering breath she took. She delivered each note with earnest love.

~~~

The salt-encrusted boathouse door shook when Halvor knocked. He struck it with a confidence he did not feel and when it opened, his heart gave way with it. Seated at the old table were not only the three Big Men he expected, but also the hooded Belgr and the Man of Stone, Steinarr. All were well-known in the town. They had a certain reputation. As Halvor stood, hesitating, Sly-Erik spoke.

"So, Halvor, you have arrived at last!"

"Indeed, he has."

"Told you he'd come…"

"I CAN BASH HIM IF YOU WANT, I CAN!"

"Shh…"

Halvor took a deep breath and plunged into conversation. This had to work. There was no turning back.

"Sly-Erik, I-I am d-delighted to be here," he lied, inclining his head in mock respect. "I have thought long and hard about the meeting with the towns-people, and I f-feel I was in the wrong."

Tap. Tap. Tap.

"I r-realise that the people have to eat and that you are the one man who can deliver the w-whale to them."

Tap. Tap. Tap.

"I would like to offer my services to you, on board your fine v-vessel, and assure you that I am your most humble servant."

Halvor had rehearsed this speech for hours. Fancy words did not come naturally to him and it had been hard to say things he did not mean. He swallowed nervously, hoping he had sounded convincing. The tap-tap-tapping had unnerved him somewhat.

Sly-Erik fixed Halvor with a piercing stare and scraped back his chair. With a drag and a tap, he made his way over to him and stood so that he could whisper in Halvor's ear.

"Just as well you want to join us, Halvor, because I would give you no choice. The whale is going to die and you are going to have its blood on your hands!"

Halvor blinked with each word spoken as if they had pierced him like hot needles.

"If you are involved in this too," Sly-Erik continued, "there will be no need for me to worry about anyone informing the authorities, busy-body-know-nothings that they are!" He smiled a slow smile then drag-tapped his way back to the table. He gestured that Halvor should join them.

Halvor drew the sack he was carrying, from his shoulder, and placed it in front of him.

"As – as an a-apology for speaking out against you, Sly-Erik, I have b-brought some food and drink to strengthen us before sailing."

Sly-Erik raised a sceptical eyebrow. He glanced at the suddenly eager faces around him. Belgr had removed his hood and was rubbing his wizened hands together. Steinarr had begun to squint at the sack. Valdrik, sitting next to Galmann, was having to wipe a sudden gobbet of spit from his jacket. He turned to Halvor and narrowed his eyes.

"This wouldn't be a trick, would it?" he questioned.

Halvor shook his head vehemently.

"NO! NO!" he protested, rather too quickly and loudly. Realising this was a bit of an over-reaction, he gathered himself together and continued with better control, "No, not at all, Sly-Erik!"

Halvor undid the draw-string at the neck of the sack and fumbled inside.

"Look, I have bread and fish!" So saying, he pulled out Hildi's loaf and smoked fillets. "And cheese!" Grimhildr's goats' cheese rolled onto the table. For a moment, it circled slowly, all eyes following it in disbelief, and then it finally came to rest under Steinarr's nose.

"I'LL HAVE SOME OF THAT, I WILL!" the Big Man announced and reached out a great paw to grab it.

THWACK!

Without warning, a hunting knife was thrown madly through the air. It landed with its razor-sharp point down, right smack in the middle of the cheese. It swung backwards and forwards as the squashy centre began to ooze out. Halvor looked at the Big Men around the table. He had been right; the cheese was irresistible. Even Sly-Erik was eyeing the food now.

"And," Halvor announced, producing his flagon with a flourish, "I have ale!"

There was an intake of breath from the Big Men. What a feast! Where had he got it all from? Halvor waited, fingers crossed, for Sly-Erik's reaction.

Tap. Tap. Tap.

"Food, yes," he said quietly. "Ale, no."

~~~

Grimhildr kept to the gathering shadows as she made her way along the quayside. Her poshtig clanked slightly and dragged heavily on one arm, containing as it did, a troll-axe, a stone hammer and an odd backen-scratchli lent to her by their cousin, Hairy Bogley, a while ago. She screwed her eyes up and scanned the moored boats.

So many to be seen. But which one? All seemed so still. Waiting.

The calm before the storm.

There were large boats and small boats. There were boats with peeling paint and others with rusted anchors. There were old boats and new boats. Boats for fishing, boats for sailing.

Which one? Which one?

Then, Grimhildr allowed a slow smile of relief to spread across her furrowed brow. Of course! There! Just a short way along from the boathouse.

The vessel was the only one which looked as if it had been tended to recently. Its prow faced the open water and was easily the largest to be seen. The ropes were not frozen in their coils. The decks had fresh boot prints showing a day's worth of deadly preparation. The windows of the cabin were scraped clear of the winter's frost and thick snow. Stacked neatly were sharp spikes on long sticks, polished and free from the tarnish of neglect. Without doubt, this great beast was the very boat which would be taken out onto the fjord in order to hunt the whale.

A pale amber light leaked out of a chink in the boathouse frame. It gave little away but was enough to tell Grimhildr that the Big Men were inside, putting their last minute plans together. They would be waiting for the right time to set sail, pulling on waterproof clothing and huge boots. She looked from the boathouse to the grey craft resting at the harbour's edge. She would have to start her sabotage quickly – and not worry about the noise – because she couldn't be sure how much time she had.

Using her hickory stick to steady herself, Grimhildr climbed aboard.

~~~

The rye bread had been ripped apart into greedy hunks. The cheese had been stabbed in a sudden frenzy and scraped across the filthy table. The smoked fish had been fought over until Belgr, who could count, managed to convince Steinarr that there was one for each of them. The Big Men gobbled and belched their way through the feast. Halvor saw Sly-Erik wipe his mouth and sit back on his throne-like chair. Had he eaten his fill? Was he ready to give the order to weigh anchor and venture out to sea?

Halvor had to act.

The Big Men just *had* to drink the Shloopish.

Shaking in his boots and warily watching Sly-Erik, Halvor swept the flagon of ale up in his hand and held it aloft.

"A toast to Njord!" he announced grandly. "Viking god of the sea! To bring us all good luck in our hunt!"

The Big Men thumped their fists and cheered.

"YES! YES!" they boomed. "A TOAST TO NJORD!"

Halvor grinned widely at them in false friendship, his face flushed with hope, but almost as soon as the words were out of his mouth, Sly-Erik was on his feet.

"NO!" he thundered.

All fell ominously silent. The Big Men looked suddenly sheepish, like scolded children. Sly-Erik glared at Halvor and lowered his voice menacingly.

"I said, **'no ale'**."

Tap. Tap. Tap.

"Now finish your food. We set sail soon."

~~~

A cold breeze accompanied the first darkness of the evening as the swell of the water changed. Mistig Vorter became slacker to row and the current began to pull its tiny frame towards the open sea. Thom, realising they could be carried away against their will, struggled with the oars to keep the little boat where he wanted it. He suddenly had to fight hard against the tide.

"Wass mattoori, Thom?" Dotta cried out in anguish, feeling the change in course.

"Es verisht trickoori, Dotta!" Thom called against the biting wind, digging his furry feet down hard to get a firmer grip. "Dee vorter es strongish! Peepors pleasor!"

Dotta knew she must not concern herself with the boat. She had to leave that to Thom. She gathered her goat hair blanket ever more closely around her shoulders as the wind flicked her hair viciously, stinging her desperate face. Where was the young minke? Surely he must hear her. The change in current meant that the time was right for the Big Men to set sail. Dotta searched the dark surface for a sign; a breach, a blow. She could see nothing.

"Pleasor, littelor walloo!" she begged. "Comli, comli!"

Once more, she placed her pipes to her chattering lips and blew her best whale song.

The cruel wind laughed at the little trolls, in the precariously rocking boat, and whipped the notes away from the pipes. They were tossed from wave to wave, thrown into the air and scattered randomly out of tune into the gathering dusk.

~~~

With a *clang!* Grimhildr emptied her tools on to the deck. She too had felt the change in the wind and wave direction and knew this signalled the time to set sail. At any moment, the Big Men could come thundering down the path from the boathouse and find her. Would Halvor be able to delay them? Would the Shloopish work?

The she-troll grunted with exertion as she pulled at the ship's wheel. It was not going to budge. Without wasting time to think, Grimhildr reached for the nearest tool. Her stone hammer was a loyal friend and, gripping it firmly, she whacked at the wheel with as much force as she could muster. Again and again she struck – **Bang! Clang!** – but the wood did not give way. The hammer seemed to bounce off each time.

"Fastli, Grimhildr! Fastli!" she muttered to herself, looking down at the other tools which lay at her feet. The axe! Of course! Her trusty wood-chopper!

Dropping the hammer, Grimhildr grabbed the troll-axe and raised it above her head. Throwing caution to the biting wind around her, she yelled as she gave a fearsome blow – **SMACK!**

"Foor dee walloo!" she cried, as splinters of wheel began to fly through the air in every direction. Over and over again she raised her axe and crashed it down upon the ship's wheel. **Thwack! Crack! Smack!** It lay in broken pieces at her hairy troll-feet.

Grimhildr paused, panting for a moment. What else could she do? The Big Men could replace a ship's wheel easily. There might even be one in the boathouse for all she knew. There *had* to be something else she could do to stop them from sailing. As she stepped back to admire the damage, one foot nudged the backen-scratchli tool from Bogley. It had a wooden pear-shaped handle attached to a long metal piece. Grimhildr bent down to pick it up. As she did so, her eyes fell on the power handle for the boat. It was a simple forward-backward shift stick which moved in a slot. A-hah! With a hard thrust, the metal backen-scratchli was forced into the slot, deep down into the workings of the power box itself. The wooden handle broke off with the force of the action, leaving the metal part unseen, but jamming any movement of the shift stick. Perfect!

Now to collect her troll tools and leave…

… "Foor dee walloo!"

~~~

Halvor was beginning to panic. The Big Men had almost finished eating and Sly-Erik was barking instructions. If they didn't drink Dotta's special sleeping potion, there was every chance they would leave the boathouse in minutes, ready to hunt the whale, with Halvor as an accomplice. He was horrified that he might have to join them after all and play his own part in this deadly venture. He thought of his troll friends. It was sickening that they might fail to protect the minke after all their efforts.

Sly-Erik raised a hand for silence.

"Enough of your greed! The time is right. The wind blows in our favour and Njord has turned the tide. We must leave without delay if we are to succeed in our mission!"

The Big Men began to get to their feet. Steinarr cast a last look down the length of the table. All the food had been eaten, except for a small piece of bony fish which Belgr had left. As the others went to gather their outdoor clothing and great boots, Steinarr snaffled the fish and shoved it into his mouth.

"I BELIEVE IN WASTE-NOT-WANT-NOT, I DO!" he tried to explain with his mouth stuffed. He took another breath to say something else, but suddenly began to cough – and then to splutter – and then to *choke*, his face becoming red and his squinting eye bulging in panic.

"He can't breathe! Someone do something!"

"He's choking!"

"Indeed, he is! What a pity."

Sly-Erik began to thump Steinarr's back, dislodging a stuck fish bone and Halvor saw his chance. In a second he had reached for his flagon of ale and darted across the room. Pulling Steinarr's head back by his hair, he poured the Shloopish and ale mixture down the Big Man's throat. The liquid sloshed down Steinarr's chin as he gasped and gulped.

"MORE! MORE!"

Halvor obliged.

As the others watched, a daft grin began to spread across Steinarr's face. He looked much better and decidedly relaxed.

"Ahem, ahem!" coughed Belgr, unconvincingly. "I think I must have a fish bone caught slightly too..." and he reached for the drink, taking a huge gulp before Sly-Erik could stop him.

"And me! And me!" Valdrik exclaimed snatching the flagon from Belgr's grasp.

It didn't take long for Galmann to follow suit. He looked so wild that nobody was even going to ask if he had a fish bone stuck. The flagon of Shloopish was passed from one to the other in quick succession, until it was finally drained dry. The Big Men began to sway on their feet. Then, when they tried to reach the door of the boathouse, they began to stagger. Then, one-by-one, they slumped to the floor.

A tumultuous snoring set up.

All had drunk the Shloopish except for Halvor.

And –

Sly-Erik.

He didn't look at all pleased.

"It appears the job is left to us then, my clever friend," Sly-Erik snarled at Halvor. "Let the other fools sleep. You will come with me!"

Halvor opened his mouth to protest.

Then he remembered Kishi.

~~~

Trusting instinct ~

Snatches of sound danced on the surface of the water. The notes hopped and jumped between splashes and swells.

The minke stirred in the depths.

Could it be?

Dare he follow?

Over and over, up and under, the notes persisted in calling him. Their familiar sound comforted him. He felt calmer. Reassured. Encouraged.

As he rose gently from the depths to which he had sunk, the young whale felt a slight pull from the current. It was the slightest drag but he swam with it. Slowly, gradually, he brought his body closer to the surface. Trusting.

The piped song reached him at last.

It beckoned him like a child to a mother.

Chapter Ten

*D*rag – tap. Drag – tap. Drag – tap.

Sly-Erik moved with surprising speed, despite his wooden leg. Halvor was made to hurry from the boathouse, along the quayside towards the whaling boat. It loomed before them in the darkness, facing the open water, ready for its murderous mission. Halvor's mind was racing.

Had he given the trolls enough time?

Had Grimhildr managed to scupper the boat?

Had Dotta and Thom located the whale?

Grimhildr's task was a back-up plan in case the Shloopish failed. They had hoped it wouldn't be necessary, but now Halvor knew that if Grimhildr had not been strong enough, he would be sailing with Sly-Erik within minutes.

As the two Big Men reached the boat, Sly-Erik smiled. He slowed his drag–tap and turned to fix Halvor with hard eyes.

"Here's my little baby," he said with a nod of his head. "All ready for action. All ready to serve me. All ready to kill!"

Halvor did not respond.

"Dear, dear, Halvor! I thought you were keen to join me but you seem a touch reluctant."

Halvor stood still by the boat and returned Sly-Erik's stare. He said nothing.

Sly-Erik began to laugh.

"It seems your plan has failed, Halvor! Did you *really* think you could outwit *me*? You should have kept your mouth shut when you didn't agree with my plans. Your pathetic little mongrel would have been so much safer!"

Halvor clenched his fists. The thought of Kishi being in danger from Sly-Erik made his blood boil. He had no choice but to do as he was told if he were to keep her safe.

Sly-Erik spat on the ground. He regarded Halvor with disdain. He was becoming increasingly angry.

"A man who will risk his own life on a whale hunt just to save a pet dog is truly stupid! A sentimental idiot!"

Halvor flinched at the words, but kept silent.

He stood motionless in front of Sly-Erik, trying to control his feelings.

Sly-Erik tapped his leg in frustration. This speechless fool in front of him had wrecked his whaling team and come close to sabotaging the whole scheme. The towns-people needed food, and he needed power. This was Sly-Erik's great opportunity. He wanted to frighten Halvor, to get some reaction out of him. He raised his voice to shout:

"IF YOU WANT YOUR FOUR-LEGGED FRIEND TO KEEP HER FOUR LEGS, YOU'D BETTER GET ON BOARD – AND FAST!"

It was at this minute that a shadow moved.

A short, dumpy shadow brandishing a shadowy stick.

Before Sly-Erik knew what was happening, Grimhildr had burst out from her hiding place on the quayside and whacked Sly-Erik's wooden leg with her hickory stick.

Ker-whack!

His leg scooted out from under him and the Big Man lost his balance, dropping to the ground, completely pole-axed.

"HOW DARE YOU THREATEN OUR DOG!" Grimhildr bellowed furiously, and proceeded to bash him with her stick. "FIRST YOU WANT TO KILL THE WHALE, AND THEN YOU WANT TO HURT OUR DOG!"

Bash! Bash!

"TAKE THAT!"

Bash!

"AND THAT!"

Bash! Bash!

Sly-Erik rolled around on the floor, covering his head with his hands and squawking with fright. He didn't seem to be able to avoid the beating stick and he certainly couldn't get to his feet.

Halvor looked on with concern.

"Grimhildr! STOP!" he exclaimed. "You'll really hurt him! You mustn't, no matter how angry you feel!"

Grimhildr hesitated for a moment, holding her hickory stick aloft. Her white hair was blowing about her head and her eyes were bright with wicked amusement. She grinned at Halvor.

"AND THAT!" she roared, just catching Sly-Erik's look of disbelief as her last bash sent him rolling off the quayside and into the freezing fjord water with a *splash!*

Halvor ran to the water's edge and peered down. A stream of bubbles was rising in a long line up to the surface. But Sly-Erik could not be seen. Without a moment's delay, he threw off his coat and gloves, and pulled off his great boots.

"Whatever are you doing?" Grimhildr asked, slapping her hands together in satisfaction at a job well done.

"I'M GOING IN!"

Grimhildr was puzzled.

"Why do you want to do that?"

"HE CAN'T SWIM! HE HAS A WOODEN LEG!"

"So? I've wrecked his boat – now I'm wrecking him!"

"WE CAN'T LET HIM DROWN!"

Grimhildr was incredulous. She shook her head in amazement as Halvor dived into the water and disappeared from view.

He was such a good Big Man.

He was such a foolish Big Man.

~~~

Mistig Vorter unexpectedly began to rock madly from side-to-side. There appeared to be a great swell forcing the little boat to rise and fall dangerously, sweeping it upwards and then crashing it down.

Dotta gripped the sides of the wooden craft in alarm.

"THOM!" she shouted in sudden panic, "WASS HAPPENIG, THOM? HELPEN! HELPEN MEER! PLEASOR, HELPEN MEER!"

The boat lunged and Thom struggled to keep balance as he stretched out a hairy arm, desperately trying to hold Dotta. As she reached out her hand to clasp his, she suddenly screamed in dismay –

"THOM! MI PEEPORS! MI PEEPORS!"

Thom looked on in horror as the precious wooden pipes fell from Dotta's grasp and a curling wave flipped them overboard, down into the churning water.

"NAY, DOTTA! NICS DEE PEEPORS!"

Gone. Forever.

~~~

Halvor heaved the spluttering form of Sly-Erik onto the quayside. Both Big Men were drenched and their clothes clung icily to their gasping bodies. Halvor bent over his enemy, hands on knees, taking great gulps of air. They were lucky to be alive. It would have been impossible to survive for more than a few minutes in water so cold. Without Halvor, and unable to swim to save himself, Sly-Erik would have perished quickly. Halvor had been both strong and courageous. Grimhildr was nowhere to be seen.

"W-w-where is sh-she?" Sly-Erik asked, his teeth chattering uncontrollably.

"Who?"

"The m-mad t-t-troll!"

"What are you talking about, Sly-Erik? There is no troll here," replied Halvor. He knew that, in her rage, Grimhildr had forgotten herself and bashed the Big Man over and over again. And Sly-Erik was not someone to upset.

"You m-must have seen her!" Sly-Erik insisted, still wheezing as he sucked in the night air. "She came out of the shadows and w-w-whacked me! The m-mad t-troll w-whacked me right into the water! W-wait till I get her!"

Halvor shook his head.

"You are wrong, Sly-Erik," he answered, trying to keep his own voice steady and reassuring. "There is no troll here. You slipped on some seaweed, that's all!"

"Seaweed? SEAWEED? As if I did!"

"That's exactly what you did, Sly-Erik."

Sly-Erik looked up at Halvor suspiciously. He must have seen the she-troll. He *did* see the she-troll! Sly-Erik remembered hearing Halvor telling the troll to stop. Why was he pretending there had been no troll? No fight? No repeated bashings with that sturdy, gnarled stick?

Halvor reached down to the slumped figure at his feet and pulled him up by his dripping jacket collar. He stared straight into Sly-Erik's eyes, lowering his voice to a whisper.

"Think about it, oh Sly-One. You know you cannot get the whale. You have no crew and your whaling boat has been scuppered."

Sly-Erik wriggled to try to free himself from Halvor's grasp. He was too weak. He could only whimper and shake his head in denial.

"No, no!" he whined. "Not my boat!"

"Oh yes," replied Halvor grimly. "So, with no whale and no boat, you are not going to look good in the towns-people's eyes, are you?"

Sly-Erik moaned in despair. Halvor continued.

"So are you *really* going to admit to them that a she-troll got the better of you? That a she-troll whacked you into the water? That you, Sly-Erik, the descendant of such an important whaling family, were felled by a troll one-half your size?"

Sly-Erik shook his head and now made no further attempt to struggle.

"I think, Sly-Erik," Halvor carried on, "your best story, if you are asked, is that you slipped with your wooden leg on some seaweed. You need to get as far away as possible before you are found out! The troll is long-gone. You are no match for her."

Sly-Erik stared back at Halvor. How had this happened? His plan for fame and power had slipped away from him, so suddenly and so completely. He had been defeated by this man and a troll. He heaved a long sigh.

"I suppose I should thank you for saving my life," he muttered darkly.

Halvor said nothing. He released his strong grip from the other man's collar and steadied him on his wooden leg. Sly-Erik continued.

"I suppose you want me to say, 'Oh, thank you, Halvor!'" Sly-Erik put on a high-pitched sing-song voice. "Thank you for being so bwave and big and stwong, and saving me from certain death in the nasty cold water!"

Halvor began to turn away. He was sick of Sly-Erik and did not want to hear any more from him, not even a thank you. Sly-Erik stood, looking dejectedly out to sea.

"You know what, Halvor?" he questioned. "You know what?"

"What?"

"I *don't* thank you. Oh, no, I do *not* thank you. I would far rather you *hadn't* saved me."

Halvor looked back at him, puzzled.

"I would have far rather drowned in those cold, dark depths than carry this burden of shame. I do not deserve the Sly family name."

Fleetingly, as Halvor looked at his old foe, he felt a moment of sympathy. Then he remembered Kishi. And the whale. And his true friends, the trolls.

He turned and walked away.

~~~

The reason for the water's turbulence suddenly became clear. As Mistig Vorter was tossed about, one second plunging downwards, the next rising high on a rollercoaster ride of waves, the reason for it all became quite beautifully clear.

The young minke whale breached at last!

He broke the surface of the water just in front of the trolls' tiny boat, blowing and breathing, showering them with spray. It seemed to the trolls that he looked straight at them.

Dotta and Thom could not believe their eyes. They clasped each other tightly and gazed in wonderment at the majesty of the creature before them. He had heard the pipe song after all! He had followed Dotta's tune.

Tears of joy and relief ran down her beaming face.

The whale arched and dived, flashing the white diamond of his flipper patch as he disappeared from view.

~~~

The next day dawned peacefully. The sky was a clear, ice-blue and the bright winter sun sprinkled sparkles on the water, trees and snow. In the town, the Big People had stirred from their night's slumber. Their first thought had been that of the whale and everyone, as they awoke, had looked from their windows across the fjord.

All was still.

One-by-one, they gathered at the quayside to scan the water and talk.

"His boat's still here, you know," one muttered darkly to his neighbour. "It's in a bit of a state."

"Odd, that," came the reply.

"No sign of any whale," another commented gloomily.

"No sign of Sly-Erik either," someone responded.

The fjord lay quietly in front of them.

As the minutes ticked by, the crowd grew more restless. This calm morning was not what they had been expecting. This silence was not what they had been hoping for. They had expected to have been awoken – perhaps in the middle of the night – by eager shouts and the triumphant hooting of the whaling boat's siren! They had expected a flurry of activity down in the harbour as Sly-Erik and his crew laboured to bring their quarry ashore. They had expected men to rush with ropes and knives, each one bawling instructions at the others; the thrill and the noise of a successful slaughter should have been theirs. Every man, woman and child had been expecting glorious *excitement!*

Not this stillness.

A single voice broke through.

"So where are they? Where are Sly-Erik's men? Where is Sly-Erik? What have they done with the whale?"

"The boathouse!" another cried. "Let's try the boathouse!"

As one, the crowd turned away from the water's edge and surged along the harbour wall in the direction of Sly-Erik's meeting place. Women held back their children in case they got crushed, such was the throng of fuming Big Men.

When the boathouse door swung open, so did their mouths.

Before them was Sly-Erik's crew. Steinarr had just roused and he was rubbing his bleary eyes, squinting and blinking at the sudden light. Belgr and Valdrik were still slumped uncomfortably on the floor, arms and legs tangled in Belgr's long, black cloak. Galmann's wild hair covered his closed eyes but fluttered slightly as he snored, spit dribbling from a corner of his mouth. The table was laid with evidence; there had been feasting here. The flagon lay empty and smashed near the door.

It was all too clear to the townsmen.

After a stunned silence as they took in the scene, great shouts of indignation and rage went up.

"They have been EATING AND DRINKING!"

"They have been STUFFING THEMSELVES whilst our children stay HUNGRY!"

"LOOK HOW THEY SLEEP!"

"NO HUNT FOR THE WHALE!"

"They've had BREAD and CHEESE and FISH!"

"No food for US!"

"HOW DARE THEY?"

As Steinarr struggled to throw off the effects of Dotta's Shloopish, the Big Men from the town barged into the room to vent their anger.

Sly-Erik's boathouse was wrecked in seconds.

~~~

The sunlight that morning had brought the promise of spring at last. Two flaggermusses hung upside down, swinging gently in a corner of a little forest shack.

Dotta hummed contentedly as she busied herself with medicines and food, animals playing at her feet. She was completely lost in happy dreaming.

Grimhildr was outside, chopping wood to make a special box-bed.

A special box-bed for a special dog.

A special dog with chocolate-brown eyes.

A special box-bed to hold some very special new arrivals.

Maybe this time Dotta would actually get to keep one for herself.

Across the fjord, Grimo stretched out along the foot of Hildi and Thom's bed, rolled onto his back and started to purr. As usual, Hildi stirred first. She smiled a gentle troll-smile.

"Gooshty morgy, Thom!" she whispered. "Varken oop."

Thom yawned and stretched. His arms were stiff and sore from rowing hard, but he felt good. He hugged his little troll-wife and kissed the top of her head.

All was well in their world.

In their troll-world.

In their love.

~~~

Freedom ~

How does it feel, then, little minke?

Can you feel the rush of the water around you?

Are you diving deep?

Are you swimming once more with your kind?

You have the ocean before you.

And the rest of your life.

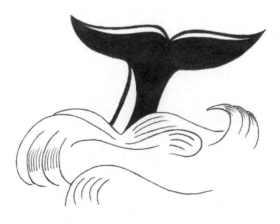